Undercover

When healing hides a deadly secret

Jordan Prescott

First Edition: November 2024

Table of Contents

Chapter 1 A Stranger in Chaos.......1

Chapter 2 Shadows Beneath the Surface.......17

Chapter 3 Into the Restricted Zone.......33

Chapter 4 Unspoken Warnings.......48

Chapter 5 Trust and Betrayal.......64

Chapter 6 Threads in the Dark.......81

Chapter 7 The Tipping Scales.......98

Chapter 8 The Cost of Secrets.......114

Chapter 9 Unraveling the Threads.......131

Chapter 10 Unmasking the Operative.......147

Chapter 11 Dangerous Revelations.......162

Chapter 12 Ethical Crossroads.......178

Chapter 13 The Walls Close In.......192

Chapter 14 The Breaking Point.......209

Chapter 15 The Final Showdown 226

Epilogue Shadows in the Light 242

Chapter 1
A Stranger in Chaos

Lily Chen hesitated for a moment as the sliding glass doors of St. Raphael's ER whooshed open. The sudden rush of cold, sterile air hit her face, but it wasn't the temperature that stopped her—it was the sound. The cacophony of ringing phones, overlapping voices barking orders, and the beeping of monitors assaulted her senses. For a moment, she simply stood there, trying to absorb it all. The sight of patients on stretchers, their faces pale with pain, doctors and nurses moving with practiced urgency, and the faint, lingering smell of antiseptic—this was her new world.

It wasn't that Lily wasn't prepared. Years of grueling med school and clinical rotations had been leading to this moment. But the reality of being here, in the chaos of one of the city's busiest emergency rooms, was a different beast entirely. Her stomach clenched as she tightened her grip on the strap of her messenger bag.

"Hey, rookie!" A voice cut through the din.

Lily turned sharply to see a woman striding toward her, her sneakers squeaking against the linoleum floor. She was in her forties, her brown hair pulled back into a tight bun, her scrubs neatly pressed but with a coffee stain on one sleeve—a sign of someone far too busy to care. She carried a clipboard under her arm like it was a part of her body.

"You must be Dr. Chen," the woman said with a grin that was equal parts welcoming and mischievous. "I'm Nina Perez, charge nurse and unofficial tour guide of this fine establishment. And by 'tour guide,' I mean you'll be lucky if I tell you where the bathrooms are."

Lily's lips quirked into a small, nervous smile. "That's me. First day. Thanks for… the welcome?"

Nina's eyes twinkled with amusement as she glanced at Lily's crisp white coat and the tightly wound bun at the nape of her neck. "You look like you just stepped out of the subway and into a war zone. Pro tip: that coat's gonna be red by the end of the night."

Lily let out a nervous laugh, tucking a loose strand of hair behind her ear. "I figured it'd be busy, but…" She gestured vaguely to the organized chaos around her.

Nina patted her shoulder with a firm hand. "This is just a warm-up, sweetheart. We haven't even hit the after-work rush yet. But don't worry. You'll either love it or cry yourself to sleep every night. Sometimes both."

Before Lily could respond, Nina's radio crackled to life. A voice came through, sharp and urgent: "Incoming trauma, ETA two minutes."

Nina nodded briskly, already in motion. "Looks like you're getting a baptism by fire. Welcome to the jungle, rookie."

Lily barely had time to process Nina's words before the nurse was halfway down the hall, barking orders at the staff. Swallowing her nerves, Lily squared her shoulders and stepped further into the ER, her sneakers squeaking slightly on the polished floor.

As she made her way to the central desk, her eyes darted around, trying to take in every detail. A teenage boy sat in one corner, clutching his wrist as his mother argued with a receptionist. A paramedic wheeled in a man on a stretcher, the metallic scent of blood trailing after them. A woman sobbed softly near the waiting room's vending machine.

The sheer weight of it all was dizzying, but Lily forced herself to stay grounded. She was here for a reason. She'd spent years working toward this moment. But as she placed her bag down at the desk and glanced at the patient board, her hands trembled slightly.

Nina's voice called out again, cutting through her thoughts. "Chen! You're up. Bed Four. Cracked rib. Should be a nice, easy start for you."

Lily blinked, her nerves surging. She quickly grabbed a stethoscope and clipboard, her footsteps faltering only slightly as she moved toward the designated bed.

When she reached it, she paused, taking in the man sitting there. He was in his early thirties, dark-haired, with a rugged yet sharp-edged appearance. His shirt was torn, revealing bruises along his ribs, but he sat upright, his posture too composed for someone in pain. His eyes were dark, intelligent, and they locked onto hers with unnerving precision.

"You're Mr. Wilde?" Lily asked, glancing at the chart.

The man's lips twitched into a faint smirk. "That's me. But let's skip the formalities. Call me Ethan."

Lily gave him a tight smile, trying to maintain her professionalism. "Alright, Ethan. Let's see what we're dealing with."

As she leaned in to examine him, her heart pounded in her chest. Ethan Wilde didn't seem like the kind of man who ended up in an ER by accident.

"You look nervous, Doc," Ethan said, his voice low and calm. "First day?"

"Is it that obvious?" Lily replied, her voice steadying as she slipped her stethoscope into her ears.

"Don't worry," he said, his smirk widening. "You'll be great. Just don't pass out on me."

She couldn't help but chuckle softly, the tension easing just a fraction. But as she pressed her hands gently against his ribs, searching for signs of further injury, she felt his sharp gaze on her. It wasn't just the look of a patient—it was the look of someone who was watching, calculating, waiting.

Lily swallowed hard, pulling back. Something told her Ethan Wilde wasn't here for just a cracked rib.

Ethan Wilde sat on the hospital bed, the thin paper crinkling beneath him as he adjusted his position. His back was straight, his shoulders squared, and his dark eyes scanned the room with a calm that felt entirely out of place in the chaos of the ER. He exuded an air of control that didn't match the bruising along his ribs or the tension in his jaw.

Lily approached hesitantly, clutching his chart in one hand and her stethoscope in the other. She glanced at the name written in neat block letters: *Ethan Wilde.* Her eyes flicked up to meet his, and for a moment, she faltered under his steady, unflinching gaze.

"You're Mr. Wilde?" she asked, her voice steady despite the nerves prickling at her skin.

"In the flesh," Ethan replied, a faint smirk tugging at the corner of his mouth. His tone was light, almost playful, but his eyes betrayed a sharpness, as though he were sizing her up.

Lily cleared her throat, shifting her weight slightly. "I'm Dr. Chen. I'll be taking care of you today."

"Dr. Chen," he repeated, as though testing the name on his tongue. "Alright then, Doc. What's the verdict? Am I going to live?"

Her lips twitched into a small, professional smile. "I'll have to examine you first before I make any promises."

"Fair enough." He leaned back slightly, wincing as he did. "But let's get one thing straight—if I don't survive, I'm blaming you."

Lily chuckled softly, her nerves easing a fraction. "I'll do my best to avoid that." She moved closer, setting the clipboard down and slipping the stethoscope into her ears. "So, Ethan, what happened?"

"Bar fight," he said casually, his voice tinged with amusement.

Lily arched an eyebrow, pressing the stethoscope gently against his chest. "Bar fight? That's a bit cliché, isn't it?"

He smirked, his gaze unwavering. "What can I say? I'm a walking stereotype. Tough crowd, too."

"Tough enough to crack a rib?" she asked, tilting her head as she moved the stethoscope to his side.

"Guess so."

His answers were short, deliberately vague. Lily tried to focus on her examination, but her mind kept circling back to his tone, the way his words felt measured, as though he were choosing them carefully.

"Any trouble breathing?" she asked.

"Just the usual when someone punches you in the ribs," he replied lightly.

Lily pulled the stethoscope away and stepped back slightly. "Your vitals are stable, but I'll need to order an X-ray to confirm the fracture."

Ethan nodded, but his eyes lingered on her longer than she expected. "First day?"

She blinked, caught off guard. "Is it that obvious?"

"Just a hunch," he said, shrugging with one shoulder. "You've got that look about you—wide-eyed but determined. Like you're waiting for someone to tell you you're doing alright."

Lily frowned, feeling the warmth of embarrassment creep into her cheeks. "I'm perfectly capable of handling myself."

"Didn't say you weren't," Ethan replied smoothly, his smirk softening into something closer to genuine. "Just making an observation."

"Well, here's an observation," Lily shot back, crossing her arms. "You don't seem like the kind of person who gets into bar fights."

Ethan chuckled, the sound low and dry. "And what kind of person do I seem like, Doc?"

She hesitated, searching for the right words. "I'm not sure yet. But you don't strike me as someone who goes looking for trouble."

"Maybe trouble just finds me," he said quietly, his voice dropping to a near whisper.

The words hung in the air between them, heavier than she expected. Lily opened her mouth to respond, but before she could, Ethan shifted slightly, wincing again as he adjusted his position.

"You alright?" she asked, stepping forward instinctively.

"Just a cracked rib," he said, brushing off her concern with a faint smile. "I've had worse."

There it was again—that tension beneath the surface, the hint of something unspoken. Lily's stomach tightened as she picked up the clipboard.

"I'll order that X-ray and come back with the results," she said, her tone clipped.

Ethan nodded, watching her with that same unnerving gaze. "Looking forward to it."

She turned to leave, but his voice stopped her just as she reached the curtain.

"Hey, Doc?"

Lily glanced over her shoulder.

"Keep your eyes open in this place," he said, his tone suddenly serious. "You never know what you might see."

Lily frowned, unsure how to respond. She lingered for a moment before nodding and stepping out of the room. His words echoed in her mind as she moved down the hallway, the weight of them lingering like a shadow.

Lily hunched over the nurse's station, her pen tapping absently against the edge of her clipboard. The chart in front of her blurred as her mind replayed her encounter with Ethan Wilde. His cryptic tone, the way his dark eyes seemed to pierce through her defenses—it was all still gnawing at her.

"Earth to Dr. Chen," Nina's voice cut through the fog, sharp and teasing.

Lily startled, blinking rapidly as she turned toward the charge nurse. "Sorry, what?"

Nina leaned against the counter, her arms crossed, her smirk as sharp as a scalpel. "You're already zoning out on your first day? That's gotta be some kind of record."

"I'm fine," Lily said quickly, flipping the chart closed.

Nina's eyes narrowed playfully. "Uh-huh. Let me guess—it's Bed Four, isn't it?"

"Bed Four?" Lily repeated, feigning ignorance.

"Oh, don't play dumb," Nina said, nudging her with an elbow. "That guy—the one with the smirk and the movie-star jawline? Ethan something?"

Lily rolled her eyes, trying to keep her expression neutral. "It's just a patient, Nina."

Nina snorted. "Sure, he's just a patient. And I'm just here for the snacks." She leaned closer, her voice dropping conspiratorially. "Come on, you can admit it. He's got that whole 'bad boy with a secret' vibe going. Bet he's the type to get into all kinds of trouble—and somehow talk his way out of it."

"I'm pretty sure he's not my type," Lily replied dryly, but her cheeks betrayed her with a faint flush.

"Oh, please." Nina straightened, clearly delighted by the reaction. "You've got that look. The one that says, 'I don't trust him, but I kind of want to know why.'"

Lily sighed, glancing back at Ethan's chart. "He's… odd. There's something about him that doesn't add up."

"Odd, huh?" Nina said, her teasing tone softening just slightly. "You think he's hiding something?"

"I don't know," Lily admitted, her fingers brushing the edge of the clipboard. "He's too calm. Like he's in control of everything, even here. And the way he talks—it's like he's playing some kind of game."

"Sounds like you've been thinking about him a lot," Nina teased again, though her expression had grown more thoughtful.

Lily groaned. "Can we not make this a thing?"

"Fine, fine," Nina said, raising her hands in mock surrender. "But seriously, Lily, don't let him distract you. Guys like that? They're trouble, plain and simple. The ER's chaotic enough without you getting caught up in someone else's drama."

Lily nodded, even as her mind refused to let go of the image of Ethan's smirk—or his warning. *Keep your eyes open.*

Nina studied her for a moment longer before softening. "Look, rookie," she said, her tone shifting to something more genuine. "I get it. First days are tough. You're trying to prove yourself, keep up with the pace, and now you've got this guy throwing you off balance. But you're good. You'll find your footing."

"Thanks," Lily said quietly, appreciating the shift in tone.

"Just don't let the Ethan Wildes of the world get in your head," Nina added with a wink. "Patients like that come and go, but your focus? That's what'll get you through the day."

Lily nodded again, trying to let the words sink in. But as Nina moved off to handle another patient, the unease lingered. Ethan wasn't just distracting—he was unsettling. There was something about him that didn't fit, like a puzzle piece jammed into the wrong place.

Her eyes drifted back to the closed curtain of Bed Four. She couldn't see him, but she could feel the weight of his presence, as if he were still watching her, even from a distance.

Don't let him distract you, she told herself firmly, turning back to her charts. But as she scribbled notes on a new patient, Nina's words echoed in her mind.

Lily gathered her clipboard and stepped toward the curtain of Bed Four, ready to move on to her next patient. She had spent longer with Ethan than she intended, and her inner monologue nagged her to pick up the pace. First days in the ER weren't supposed to include lingering conversations with mysterious patients.

But before she could pull the curtain aside, Ethan's voice stopped her.

"Keep your eyes open, Doc."

She froze mid-step, her back stiffening as the words settled in the space between them. His voice wasn't loud, but it carried a weight that pressed on her chest like a hand. Slowly, she turned back to face him.

"What did you say?"

Ethan leaned forward slightly, resting his arms on his knees. The movement made him wince, but the expression that followed wasn't one of pain—it was deliberation. "This place… there's more going on than you think."

Lily frowned, gripping the clipboard tighter. "What's that supposed to mean?"

"It means," Ethan said, his tone slow and deliberate, "you're smart. You'll figure it out."

Her frustration bubbled to the surface, and she stepped closer. "Look, if you have something to say, just say it. None of this cryptic nonsense. I don't have time for games."

Ethan's smirk returned, faint and fleeting, but it didn't reach his eyes. "Games? You think I'm playing games?"

"I think you're enjoying this far too much," she shot back, her tone sharper than she intended. "The way you're acting—dropping hints, avoiding direct answers—it's not helping."

Ethan tilted his head, studying her with that unsettling focus she was beginning to recognize. "Let me ask you something, Doc," he said quietly. "Have you noticed anything… unusual around here?"

Lily blinked. "Unusual?"

"You've been here, what, a few hours?" Ethan continued, his voice soft but insistent. "And already you've got that look. Like something's not adding up."

She opened her mouth to argue, but the words died on her lips. He wasn't entirely wrong. There was a tension in the ER, a feeling she couldn't quite put her finger on. It wasn't just the chaos or the endless flow of patients—it was something beneath the surface, like an undercurrent pulling at her.

"I think," she said cautiously, "that I don't know enough yet to make that kind of judgment."

Ethan nodded slowly, as if her response was exactly what he expected. "Fair enough. But keep watching. You'll see."

Lily exhaled sharply, trying to shake off the unease creeping up her spine. "If you have concerns about this hospital or its staff, you should talk to someone in charge. Dr. Harlow—"

Ethan's laugh cut her off, low and humorless. "Harlow? Yeah, good luck with that."

"What's that supposed to mean?" she demanded.

Ethan's smirk faded completely, leaving his face unreadable. "It means you're not going to get answers from him. Trust me, Lily."

The use of her name caught her off guard. He hadn't called her that before—not "Doc" or "Dr. Chen," but Lily. It sounded too familiar, too deliberate, and it sent a shiver through her.

"Mr. Wilde—"

"Ethan," he corrected smoothly.

"Ethan," she said firmly. "If there's something wrong here, if you know something, you need to be clear about it. Vague warnings aren't going to help anyone."

He leaned back, his movements slow and careful, and let out a soft sigh. "Some things, Doc, you have to see for yourself. Otherwise, you won't believe them."

Her jaw tightened, the frustration bubbling back. "You're not making this any easier for me."

"Didn't say I would." He met her gaze, his expression unreadable once again. "But I will say this: stay sharp. Not everything is what it seems."

Lily opened her mouth to respond, to press him for more, but the sharp beep of a monitor nearby interrupted her train of thought. A nurse called her name from the other end of the ER, snapping her attention away.

She turned toward the commotion, her instincts kicking in. When she glanced back, Ethan was sitting there, his posture relaxed as if he hadn't just upended her focus.

She shook her head and stepped out of the curtained area, her grip on the clipboard tightening. It was easy to dismiss his words as paranoia, or maybe the ramblings of someone in pain. But the unease clung to her like a shadow, refusing to let go.

As she moved on to the next patient, his voice echoed in her mind. *Keep your eyes open.*

Chapter 2
Shadows Beneath the Surface

Lily rounded the corner of the third-floor hallway, her pace slowing as she spotted a familiar figure leaning against the wall near the restricted Infectious Disease wing. Her pulse kicked up, the unease from the previous night stirring up again.

"Ethan?" she called, her voice barely masking the surprise.

He looked up, a casual smile slipping into place as if he'd been waiting for her all along. "Dr. Chen. Fancy meeting you here."

She approached, crossing her arms. "You're a long way from the ER."

Ethan shrugged, glancing around as if the plain beige walls of the restricted wing were the most fascinating thing he'd seen all day. "Just got a little turned around on my way back from the restroom. This place is a maze."

Lily's eyes narrowed. "Turned around? You were admitted on the first floor, Ethan. The bathrooms aren't exactly…up here."

He chuckled, running a hand through his hair. "Guess I'm a little worse at directions than I thought. Thanks for the heads-up, Doc. I'll head back."

But she stepped into his path before he could make a move. "Hold on. You shouldn't be here. This wing is restricted for a reason. Only authorized personnel are allowed past that door," she said, nodding toward the sign clearly marked "Authorized Personnel Only."

Ethan's expression didn't falter. Instead, he flashed that disarming smile again. "And here I was, thinking you were just glad to see me."

"Ethan," she pressed, her voice serious now, "this isn't a joke. I could lose my job just by letting you stay here."

He sighed, the smile dimming slightly. "I get it, really. And I didn't mean to put you in a difficult spot. Like I said, I was just lost."

"Lost." She echoed the word, crossing her arms tighter. "You expect me to believe that?"

He held up his hands, a gesture of mock surrender. "Alright, alright. Maybe I was a little curious. Hospitals like these always have interesting stories, you know?"

"Curious?" Her eyebrows shot up. "This isn't a tour, Ethan. There are patients in this wing fighting infections and immune issues. They don't need outside germs."

"Duly noted," he said, nodding as if he were genuinely taking in her reprimand. "I'll be sure to keep my wandering to the ER."

But something about his nonchalant tone made her jaw clench. "You're not even supposed to be wandering at all. You're here to recover, not to snoop around."

He let out a low laugh, stepping just a bit closer, lowering his voice. "You're good at this, Dr. Chen. Really. You should consider a career in law enforcement with that attention to detail."

She didn't budge. "Why are you here, Ethan? Really."

For a brief moment, something shifted in his eyes, a flash of vulnerability she hadn't expected. But then, just as quickly, it was gone, replaced with that familiar, guarded look.

"I'm just a patient, Dr. Chen. No need for the interrogation," he said softly, his voice laced with a charm that almost—almost—made her want to believe him.

"Then act like one," she replied, not willing to back down. "Stay where you're supposed to be."

He sighed, running a hand over his face. "Alright, Doc, message received. But, between you and me, a little fresh air and change of scenery does wonders for a guy's recovery."

"You know what does wonders? Following the rules." She bit back a smile, knowing full well she'd used the same line on plenty of other patients. But something about Ethan made it harder to keep a straight face.

He grinned, that charm turning up a notch. "Duly noted, Dr. Chen. Anything else I should know?"

She tried to stay firm, but the slight edge of playfulness in his tone chipped away at her resolve. "Maybe…just try not to get 'lost' again. If Nina catches you up here, she won't be half as forgiving."

"Noted. Last thing I need is Nurse Nina giving me the boot." He chuckled, taking a step back toward the main hallway, giving her a casual salute as he passed. "Catch you later, Doc."

But as he turned, a strange feeling settled in her chest. This man was far from the standard patient, and no matter how easygoing his charm seemed, there was something guarded, something hidden beneath his casual bravado.

"Ethan," she called after him, her tone losing the hint of humor. "If there's something you're not telling me, if there's anything about why you're here that's…more complicated than you're letting on, I need to know."

He stopped, glancing back over his shoulder, his face half-cast in shadow. For a brief moment, she saw something in his eyes that looked almost like regret.

"You're a smart one, Dr. Chen," he murmured, his voice low. "But maybe some things are better left…unsaid."

Before she could press further, he turned and walked away, leaving her in the hallway with nothing but his cryptic words and her own rising suspicion.

Lily sat at the nurse's station, a stack of patient files open in front of her, skimming through pages of notes. The hum of the

ER had quieted to a murmur in the late afternoon, giving her a rare moment to catch up. As her eyes moved over the pages, she began noticing something unsettling: three cases in a row had similar symptoms—fever, respiratory issues, fatigue. Too similar.

"Three patients, all admitted in the past two days, all with the same symptoms," she muttered, flipping through the pages faster now.

Nina walked over, arching an eyebrow. "Talking to yourself again, Chen?"

Lily glanced up, her expression serious. "Look at this, Nina. These patients—they all have fevers, cough, fatigue. It's not flu season, and none of them have any prior conditions that would make them this susceptible."

Nina scanned the files, her brow furrowing. "Hmm. Could be a viral bug going around. Happens sometimes—one person sneezes, and before you know it, half the ward's got it."

"Maybe," Lily said slowly, chewing on her lip. "But these symptoms seem… off. There's this weird lethargy they're all experiencing. It's like they're exhausted to the bone, and it's not just from the fever. Something feels wrong."

"You're sounding a little paranoid," Nina replied, though her voice held a note of concern. "But hey, I'm just a nurse. Maybe you should run it by Dr. Harlow if you're that worried."

Lily nodded, glancing toward the hallway where she knew Dr. Harlow's office was. "I think I will. Something about this just doesn't sit right."

A few minutes later, she knocked on Dr. Harlow's door, files clutched tightly to her chest.

"Come in," came his brisk voice, laced with impatience.

She opened the door, finding him behind his desk, reading a thick medical journal. "Dr. Harlow? I need to talk to you about some of the new patients we've admitted."

He looked up, clearly disinterested. "What is it, Chen?"

She took a steadying breath, hoping her concern would come through. "I've noticed a pattern in several recent cases—high fevers, respiratory symptoms, and an unusual level of fatigue. Three patients, all within the past two days. It's not typical for this time of year, and it doesn't quite match any common viruses we see."

Harlow sighed, barely looking up from his journal. "It's a hospital, Dr. Chen. People get sick, infections spread. It's part of the job."

"I know that," she replied, resisting the urge to sound defensive. "But this isn't the usual kind of spread. There's something about the lethargy in particular—it doesn't fit the symptoms we'd expect from a normal infection."

He closed his journal, finally giving her his full attention. "So, what are you suggesting? That we're dealing with some sort of... epidemic?"

"I don't know," she admitted, trying to keep her tone measured. "I'm not suggesting anything that dramatic. But I think we should investigate. At least run some cultures, maybe get samples to the lab and see if there's a connection."

Harlow leaned back in his chair, his fingers drumming the edge of his desk. "Dr. Chen, I appreciate your enthusiasm, but this sounds like classic rookie nerves. This hospital deals with hundreds of cases like these every year."

"I get that," she said, her voice firm. "But there's something here, Dr. Harlow. These patients... they're different. I can't just ignore it."

He shook his head, looking at her with a patronizing smile. "You've been in the ER for what, a few months? Trust me, once you've worked here long enough, you'll stop seeing patterns where there are none. Focus on the patient care, not on imaginary outbreaks."

Her jaw tightened, frustration simmering beneath her professional composure. "But what if it's not imaginary? What if we miss something because we didn't look hard enough?"

Harlow sighed, his smile fading. "You're persistent, I'll give you that. Fine. I'll have a quick glance at the files, but I can't guarantee anything will come of it. If I find it's routine, that's the end of it. Understood?"

"Understood," she replied, though her gut told her it wasn't enough. She handed him the files, watching as he flipped through them with only mild interest, like he was reading the morning paper.

After a moment, he handed them back. "Looks routine to me, Dr. Chen. Viral, at worst. The best thing you can do is prescribe fluids, rest, and monitor them. No need for lab work."

"But—"

"No buts." He cut her off with a wave of his hand. "You're here to learn, Dr. Chen. So trust me when I say, there's no cause for alarm. Now, if you don't mind, I have actual work to do."

Lily bit back a retort, nodding stiffly. "Yes, Dr. Harlow. Thank you."

She turned and left the office, but the frustration lingered, thick and heavy in her chest. As she walked back to the ER, her fingers clutched the files tighter, her mind racing. Maybe Harlow was right, and maybe she was overthinking things. But something told her that these cases were more than just routine—and no amount of dismissal would shake that feeling.

Lily walked briskly down the hall, the unsettling conversation with Dr. Harlow replaying in her mind. His dismissive tone, his complete disregard for the unusual cluster of symptoms—it gnawed at her, leaving a bitter taste of frustration. She knew she should let it go, just accept that he was the expert, and that maybe she was reading too much into it. But something inside her refused to be silenced.

"Chen!" Nina's voice called out as she passed by the nurse's station, snapping her from her thoughts. "You look like you're solving world hunger over there. Everything alright?"

Lily hesitated, glancing back at Nina with a sigh. "I don't know, Nina. I talked to Dr. Harlow about these patients with fever and lethargy—the ones we admitted over the past few days?"

Nina nodded, her expression shifting to mild concern. "The ones with those weird respiratory symptoms, right?"

"Exactly," Lily said, crossing her arms tightly. "Harlow brushed it off like it was nothing. Said I was just seeing patterns where there weren't any. But… I don't know, Nina, it doesn't feel like nothing."

Nina raised an eyebrow, giving her a look that was both sympathetic and cautious. "Look, he's been here for decades. Maybe he just knows what he's doing."

"That's what I keep telling myself," Lily replied, running a hand through her hair. "But there's this gut feeling I can't shake. Something about these patients feels… off."

Nina smirked, trying to lighten the mood. "Gut feelings, huh? Not exactly what they teach us in med school."

"Yeah, well," Lily muttered, half-smiling, "sometimes it's all you've got."

Nina tilted her head, studying her. "You know, it might not be a bad idea to keep an eye on those cases. Just in case. Doesn't mean you're going against Harlow; you're just… following up."

Lily nodded, feeling a sliver of relief. "You're right. It doesn't hurt to be thorough, right?"

Nina's smile turned sly. "Exactly. You'd just be doing your job. And, besides, it's not like Harlow will notice. Half the time, he's buried in his journal."

Lily chuckled, the tension easing a bit. But as her thoughts drifted back to the patients, another memory resurfaced—Ethan, wandering around the same area as one of those patients just yesterday.

She looked at Nina, her face serious again. "There's something else… I caught Ethan Wilde wandering near one of the restricted areas yesterday. He said he was lost, but he was so close to the Infectious Disease wing."

Nina raised an eyebrow, clearly intrigued. "What was he doing up there? Thought he was just here for a cracked rib."

"That's what he says," Lily replied, her tone laced with suspicion. "But he's been anything but a typical patient. I don't know, Nina, maybe I'm overthinking this, but I can't help but wonder if he's… involved somehow."

"Involved? How?" Nina's eyes widened, leaning in closer.

Lily shook her head, trying to keep herself grounded. "I don't know. It's probably just my imagination. But he has this way of slipping around, dodging questions, saying just enough to make me wonder if there's more going on."

Nina chuckled, clearly unconvinced. "Maybe he's just one of those mysterious types who likes to keep people guessing. Could be he's just trying to charm you, make his stay a little more… interesting."

Lily sighed, crossing her arms again. "Maybe. But I can't shake the feeling that he's hiding something. And that guy he was talking to earlier—the one in the suit. It wasn't a friendly visit, Nina."

Nina gave her a sympathetic look. "Alright, so let's say you're right. Let's say Ethan's not who he says he is. What are you going to do about it? Dig into his life story?"

Lily hesitated, the weight of Nina's question settling over her. "I… don't know. I just feel like I can't ignore it. What if there's a connection between him and these strange infections?"

Nina exhaled, giving her a soft pat on the shoulder. "Lily, you're good at what you do. You have instincts for a reason. But just be careful, okay? You don't want to find yourself tangled up in something you can't get out of."

Lily nodded, her expression thoughtful. "I know. I'll be careful. But I can't ignore this."

Nina watched her for a long moment, then nodded. "Alright. You follow your instincts. Just remember—you're not on your own here. If something's up, you've got me. And if I catch him wandering around again, I'll let you know."

Lily smiled, grateful for the support. "Thanks, Nina. I'm probably just overthinking everything, but… better safe than sorry."

Nina gave her a gentle shove. "You've got a good head on your shoulders, Dr. Chen. Don't let Dr. Harlow's indifference mess with that. If you think there's something here, don't back down."

As they parted ways, Lily couldn't shake the feeling of unease that lingered. Her instincts were screaming that something was wrong—that there was a pattern here, a connection she hadn't yet uncovered. And until she knew more, she couldn't let it go.

Lily rubbed her temples as she walked down the corridor, feeling the weight of another long shift settle on her shoulders. She was halfway to the staff lounge, ready to collapse with a cup of stale coffee, when a movement caught her eye—a flash of someone familiar at the far end of the hall.

She slowed, her gaze narrowing as she saw Ethan. He was talking to a man in a dark suit, someone who looked distinctly out of place in the hospital's fluorescent-lit corridors. The man's posture was tense, his expression obscured by shadow, but his rigid stance gave off an unmistakable air of authority.

Before she could process it, the man glanced in her direction, catching her eye for a fleeting moment. Ethan turned, and their eyes met briefly, his expression flashing with something unreadable before he quickly looked away.

Lily's pulse quickened. "Ethan?" she called, her voice hesitant as she took a step forward.

The man in the suit nodded curtly to Ethan, then disappeared down the opposite hallway, his footsteps fading swiftly. Ethan, meanwhile, didn't move, his gaze fixed on a spot just past her as though lost in thought.

When she was close enough, she cleared her throat. "I didn't expect to see you… here. Again."

Ethan's expression shifted, a cool, guarded smile settling on his face. "Dr. Chen. You're working late."

"That's the job," she replied, folding her arms. "I could say the same for you, though you're not exactly working, are you?"

He shrugged, his voice smooth as ever. "Just stretching my legs. Needed a change of scenery."

She tilted her head, her eyes narrowing as she glanced in the direction the man in the suit had gone. "Who was that?"

"Who?" he asked, a little too casually, his eyes shifting away for a split second.

Lily crossed her arms tighter, refusing to let him slip away from the question. "The man you were just talking to. He didn't look like a nurse or a doctor."

"Oh, him," Ethan replied, his tone light as if they were discussing the weather. "Just a friend. Wanted to check up on me, make sure I'm healing up."

"A friend?" she echoed, skepticism lacing her voice. "Funny, he didn't look like someone here for a friendly visit. More like… business."

He smiled, a little sharper now. "Well, everyone has different ways of showing they care, I suppose."

Lily stared at him, the strange encounter feeding her growing sense of unease. "Ethan, this doesn't add up. You're wandering around restricted areas, meeting with people who look like they walked out of a government building… all while you're supposed to be here resting. Why do I get the feeling you're hiding something?"

"Maybe because you're looking too hard, Dr. Chen," he replied, his tone soft, almost coaxing. "Sometimes, a cigar is just a cigar."

"Not in my line of work," she shot back. "You don't belong here—not in the way you're pretending to."

His eyes met hers, and for a moment, his easy demeanor cracked, something raw and unguarded slipping through. But just as quickly, he masked it with a chuckle, deflecting. "You're right. I don't. But I'm here all the same. And you—you're just a doctor, right? Doing your job?"

"Just a doctor?" She felt a surge of indignation rise up, though she kept her voice even. "My job is to keep my patients safe. So if something's going on, something I should know about, you owe it to me to tell the truth."

He hesitated, his gaze flicking toward the empty corridor where the man had disappeared. For a brief moment, it seemed like he might relent, like he was on the verge of sharing something more.

But then he shook his head, the guarded mask slipping back into place. "The truth, Dr. Chen, is a slippery thing. You may want it, but sometimes it's better not to go looking for it."

Her brow furrowed, frustration boiling beneath the surface. "What's that supposed to mean?"

"It means," he said, leaning in slightly, his voice lowering to a near whisper, "some answers come with a price. And you may not like the cost."

She took a breath, feeling the weight of his words settle over her like a cold shadow. "You're not making this any easier, Ethan. Every time I see you, there's a new question. Something feels… wrong."

He sighed, his gaze softening, but his voice stayed steady, unmoved. "Then maybe it's time to let it go. Walk away, pretend you didn't see me here, that you didn't see anything at all."

"Is that what you want?" she asked, her voice quieter now, almost pleading. "Because I can't shake the feeling that you're not here by choice—that something's pulling you into something dangerous."

He looked at her, his gaze unflinching. "I'm here because I need to be. And that's all you need to know."

Before she could respond, he turned and walked down the hallway, his figure blending into the shadows until he was out of sight, leaving her alone with more questions than she'd had before. As his footsteps faded, Lily felt a lingering sense of dread curl in her chest, like a warning she couldn't shake.

She stared at the empty hallway, the silence heavy around her. Whatever Ethan Wilde was involved in, it was far more than she'd anticipated—and she had a feeling it was only the beginning.

Chapter 3
Into the Restricted Zone

The clock above the nurse's station read 12:13 a.m., its steady ticking nearly drowned out by the hum of fluorescent lights and the occasional beep of monitors. The ER had quieted, the usual chaos subdued to a manageable hum as the night shift settled into its rhythm. Lily Chen leaned over her charts, her focus wavering as exhaustion crept in. She reached for her lukewarm cup of coffee, trying to shake the weight in her eyelids.

As she sipped, a shadow moved at the edge of her vision. She turned her head sharply, her gaze narrowing toward the dimly lit corridor leading to the Infectious Disease Wing. A figure lingered there, their movements slow and deliberate.

She set the coffee down, her heart picking up speed as she rose to her feet. It took only a few steps closer to recognize him.

"Ethan?" she called out, her voice slicing through the quiet.

The man turned, and even in the low light, she could see his face clearly. Ethan Wilde stood near the heavy steel door that marked the wing's entrance. His hands rested casually in his jacket pockets, and his lips curved into that easy, familiar smile.

"Dr. Chen," he greeted, his tone warm but measured. "Burning the midnight oil, I see."

"What are you doing here?" Lily demanded, her footsteps quickening as she closed the distance between them.

Ethan shrugged, shifting slightly but keeping his posture relaxed. "Got a little lost," he said smoothly, his eyes flicking briefly to the keypad lock beside the door.

Lily's frown deepened. "This area's restricted. Patients aren't allowed back here."

"Good thing I'm not a patient anymore," Ethan replied, tilting his head slightly.

Her stomach twisted at his nonchalant tone. There was something calculated in the way he stood, like he was trying too hard to appear casual. "You're still on the hospital's watchlist. And you don't just stumble into the Infectious Disease Wing by accident."

"Fair point," he admitted, his smirk softening. "But curiosity gets the better of me sometimes."

"Curiosity about what?" she pressed, her voice firm.

He hesitated for a moment, his gaze steady on hers. "Let's just say I have… an interest in what happens around here. It's fascinating, don't you think? The way hospitals work—so much going on behind the scenes."

Lily folded her arms, the clipboard in her hand pressing into her ribs. "You shouldn't be here. If anyone catches you—"

"Relax, Doc," Ethan interrupted, raising his hands in mock surrender. "I'm not breaking any rules. Just stretching my legs."

"Near a locked door in a restricted wing?" she countered, her tone laced with suspicion.

Ethan chuckled softly. "You're sharp, I'll give you that. But there's no harm in looking, right?"

"Looking at what?" Lily demanded, stepping closer. "Because from where I'm standing, this doesn't look innocent."

His smile faded slightly, and for the first time, she caught a flicker of something else in his expression—concern, perhaps, or a shadow of doubt. "Let's just say I like knowing where I am," he said cryptically. "It's a habit. Helps me sleep at night."

"That doesn't make any sense," Lily shot back.

"It doesn't have to," Ethan replied, his voice quiet but firm. "Not yet."

Lily's jaw tightened. "You need to leave. Now. Before someone sees you and asks questions I can't answer."

Ethan's lips twitched into a faint smirk. "Protecting me already, Doc? I'm flattered."

"This isn't a joke," she said sharply, her frustration mounting. "Whatever game you think you're playing, it's not going to end well if you get caught."

For a moment, neither of them moved. Ethan's gaze held hers, unflinching, before he finally exhaled and took a step back.

"Fair enough," he said, his tone softening. "I'll head back. But Lily?"

She froze at the sound of her name, her pulse quickening.

"Be careful," he murmured, his voice low. "Sometimes the things behind locked doors are better left alone."

Her chest tightened as he turned and walked away, his footsteps echoing down the hall. She stood there for a moment, staring at the closed door of the wing and the keypad beside it. His words lingered, wrapping around her like a warning she didn't fully understand.

When she finally returned to the nurse's station, her hands were shaking slightly. She tried to focus on her charts, but her mind was already spinning with questions. What had Ethan been doing back there? And more importantly—what wasn't he telling her?

The fluorescent lights of the nurse's station buzzed faintly as Lily sat down, her mind still circling the image of Ethan standing near the Infectious Disease Wing. She tapped her pen against her clipboard, the rhythm syncing with her quickening heartbeat.

"You look like you just saw a ghost," Nina Perez said, leaning over the counter with a smirk.

Lily glanced up, startled out of her thoughts. "I might've," she muttered, then hesitated before continuing. "That guy—Ethan Wilde—I just found him near the Infectious Disease Wing."

Nina raised an eyebrow, clearly unimpressed. "And?"

"And… he shouldn't have been there," Lily said, her tone sharper than intended. "It's restricted. Patients aren't allowed back there, especially not at this hour."

Nina chuckled, brushing a strand of hair from her face. "Oh, rookie. Patients wander all the time. You'd be amazed at the places they turn up. I once found a guy in the janitor's closet trying to make a phone call on a mop handle."

Lily didn't laugh. "This felt different. He wasn't confused, Nina. He was… looking around, like he was trying to figure something out."

Nina's amusement faded slightly, though her tone remained light. "You're reading too much into it. Trust me, you'll learn to pick your battles around here. You can't go chasing after every patient who decides to take a midnight stroll."

"But he was near the keypad for the door," Lily insisted. "It wasn't random. And he didn't seem surprised when I caught him."

Nina straightened, crossing her arms. "Alright, so what do you think he was doing? Breaking in to steal medical records? Hijacking the hospital's supply of hand sanitizer?"

"I don't know," Lily admitted, frustration lacing her voice. "But I can't just ignore it."

Nina studied her for a moment, her playful expression softening into something closer to concern. "Look, Chen, I get it. First days are overwhelming. You're trying to prove yourself, and you're hyper-aware of everything going on around you. That's normal. But don't let one weird patient derail you. We've got enough to deal with."

Lily sighed, rubbing her temple with one hand. "So, what? I just forget about it?"

"Unless he tries to get into the MRI machine or starts juggling scalpels, yeah, you let it go," Nina said firmly.

The radio on Nina's hip crackled to life, and a voice came through, calling for a nurse in another wing. "Duty calls," Nina said with a shrug as she headed off. "Relax, rookie. You're doing fine."

Lily watched her go, but the uneasy feeling remained. Ethan's calm, deliberate movements near the restricted wing played on a loop in her mind. There had been nothing casual about the way he stood there, his eyes scanning the keypad and the locked door.

She glanced down at her clipboard, the patient charts suddenly feeling like a meaningless stack of papers. Her instincts told her to say something—to escalate this to someone higher up. But who?

Her thoughts drifted to Dr. Harlow, the ER's attending physician. She had already sensed his no-nonsense demeanor during rounds earlier in the night. Would he even take her seriously? Or would he dismiss her concerns the same way Nina had?

Lily gritted her teeth, frustration mounting. If she reported Ethan, she risked looking paranoid—or worse, incompetent. But if she ignored this and something was wrong, the consequences could be far greater.

She glanced at the clock, then down the hallway where she'd last seen Ethan. The wing was quiet now, the locked door standing impassively against the low hum of the ER.

"Alright," she muttered under her breath. "I'll keep an eye on him myself."

As the decision settled in her mind, a strange sense of resolve replaced the unease. Ethan Wilde wasn't just another patient, and whatever he was doing in this hospital, Lily was determined to find out.

For now, though, she shoved her doubts aside and turned her attention back to the charts in front of her. The night was far from over, and the ER wouldn't stop for one suspicious man with a too-easy smile.

The morning shift began with the sharp contrast of golden sunlight streaming through the hospital's glass façade, an ironic backdrop to the tension simmering in the ER. Lily had barely slept after her encounter with Ethan, but there was no time for reflection now.

A wave of patients began pouring in, their symptoms eerily uniform: high fevers, shortness of breath, and debilitating fatigue. By mid-morning, the ER had reached near-capacity.

"Room Five is waiting on bloodwork," a nurse called out as she passed.

Lily nodded, her focus shifting between her clipboard and the patient in front of her. A middle-aged woman clutched the thin blanket around her shoulders, her breathing labored.

"How long have you been feeling like this?" Lily asked, her voice calm but efficient.

The woman took a shallow breath before replying, "Three days. It started with a fever, but… I thought it would pass."

Lily frowned, noting the deep rattle in her patient's chest. "Have you been around anyone sick? Family? Friends?"

The woman shook her head weakly, then winced as a coughing fit overtook her. Lily stepped back, her frown deepening. This was the fourth patient with these symptoms this morning alone. Something wasn't adding up.

As Lily moved to her next patient, a teenage boy with a fever and similar complaints, her thoughts began to coalesce into uneasy patterns. The patients weren't connected geographically. Their symptoms weren't aligning neatly with any typical seasonal virus.

By the time she reached the nurse's station to check lab results, the unease had settled like a rock in her stomach. She scanned the reports, her pen hovering over the clipboard as her mind raced.

"Dr. Chen."

The familiar voice jolted her. She turned to find Ethan standing a few feet away, leaning casually against the wall, his hands tucked into his jacket pockets. He shouldn't have been there, of course, but the staff bustled past him without a second glance, as if his presence belonged.

"What are you doing here?" she asked, irritation slipping into her tone.

"Just observing," he replied, his expression calm but his eyes sharp. "Looks like a busy morning."

"It's always busy," she said curtly, turning her attention back to her charts.

Ethan stepped closer, lowering his voice. "But not always like this, right?"

Lily's hand paused mid-note. Slowly, she turned to face him. "What are you talking about?"

He tilted his head, a faint smirk tugging at his lips. "Just an observation. Things aren't always what they seem."

Frustration bubbled up in her chest, hot and insistent. "What does that mean, Ethan? If you know something, say it. Otherwise, stop wasting my time."

He raised his hands in mock surrender. "Relax, Doc. I'm just pointing out the obvious. You're smart—you'll figure it out."

Lily stepped closer, lowering her voice to match his. "Listen, I don't have time for cryptic warnings. If you have information that can help these patients, you need to tell me now."

Ethan's smirk faded, replaced by a flicker of something unreadable. For a moment, she thought he might actually say something of substance. But then he leaned back, his posture casual once again.

"You're doing good work," he said softly. "Keep at it."

Lily clenched her fists, watching as he turned and walked away. Her heart pounded as her mind churned. There was no way this was a coincidence. Ethan knew something—she was certain of it now.

As the morning wore on, the patient count continued to rise. Lily moved through the cases with methodical efficiency, but her frustration lingered just beneath the surface. The cryptic pieces Ethan had dropped refused to settle into a coherent picture, and the growing number of patients only added to her anxiety.

By noon, she was back at the nurse's station, reviewing a lab report that offered no answers. Nina approached, handing off another chart.

"You alright, rookie?" Nina asked, her tone lighter than the question deserved.

Lily nodded tightly. "These cases… they're too similar. And the labs aren't showing anything definitive."

Nina sighed, placing a reassuring hand on Lily's shoulder. "It's flu season, Chen. Sometimes, a virus is just a virus."

But Lily couldn't shake the feeling that it wasn't that simple. She glanced toward the corridor where she'd last seen Ethan, her jaw tightening. He knew something—and for now, it felt like she was the only one who could figure out what.

The nurse's station was quieter now, the steady rhythm of the ER slowing to a manageable hum as the late morning stretched on. Lily sat hunched over her clipboard, scribbling notes for her latest patient. The data swirled in her head—fevers, respiratory distress, fatigue—symptoms that screamed of something more than a coincidence.

Her pen tapped against the edge of the clipboard as her thoughts churned. For every patient she treated, more questions piled up. The tests were inconclusive, the lab work unhelpful. And then there was Ethan Wilde—his cryptic remarks, his unnerving presence, and that irritatingly casual way he seemed to know more than he let on.

"Dr. Chen."

The familiar voice was quiet, almost startling in its closeness. Lily looked up sharply, her pen freezing mid-tap. Ethan stood a few feet away, his expression subdued but his eyes as sharp as ever.

"Mr. Wilde," she said, her tone laced with frustration. "Shouldn't you be in bed? Or at least somewhere that isn't here?"

"I could say the same about you," he replied smoothly, glancing at the chart in her hand. "Still working on those cases?"

Lily set the clipboard down and folded her arms. "What do you want?"

Ethan hesitated, his gaze flicking toward the rows of occupied beds beyond the station. His usual smirk was absent, replaced by something closer to seriousness. "Just a word of advice," he said quietly, leaning slightly closer. "Be careful where you dig."

The cryptic warning set her teeth on edge. "What does that even mean?" she asked, her voice rising slightly before she caught herself. "If you're trying to scare me, it's not going to work."

"I'm not trying to scare you," Ethan said, his voice steady. "I'm trying to help you."

"Help me?" she repeated, incredulous. "By dropping vague hints and disappearing when I ask questions? That's not help, Ethan—it's just frustrating."

His jaw tightened, and for the first time, Lily thought she saw a crack in his carefully constructed facade. "Look," he began, his tone low and measured, "you're not wrong to think something's off here. But if you push too hard, you might not like what you find."

She narrowed her eyes, her patience wearing thin. "What are you hiding?"

Ethan looked away briefly, as if weighing his next words. "I'm not hiding anything that concerns you," he said finally, though his voice lacked its usual confidence.

"That's not your call to make," she shot back, stepping closer. "You know something about what's happening here—about these patients, don't you? And instead of being upfront, you're giving me riddles. Why?"

Ethan's mouth opened slightly, but no words came out. For a moment, she thought he might actually say something of substance. Then he exhaled sharply and shook his head.

"Just… keep your eyes open," he said, the familiar phrase now carrying a weight that sent a chill down her spine.

Lily stared at him, searching his face for answers that weren't coming. "Is that all you've got?" she asked, her voice softening, tinged with exasperation. "Another warning?"

"This isn't about me, Doc," Ethan replied, his gaze locking with hers. "It's about you. You're smart, but being smart doesn't always keep you safe. Be careful."

For a brief moment, his mask slipped entirely. The confidence, the charm—it all gave way to something raw and unguarded. Was it fear? Regret? She couldn't tell.

"Why are you really here, Ethan?" she asked, her voice quieter now.

But just as quickly as the crack appeared, his facade returned. His smirk flickered back, faint and fleeting, but enough to remind her of the game he was playing. "To see how the other half lives," he said lightly, straightening his posture. "Thanks for the chat, Doc."

Lily didn't stop him as he turned and walked away, his hands sliding into the pockets of his jacket. She watched his retreating figure until he disappeared around the corner, her mind racing.

His words echoed in her head: *Keep your eyes open. Be careful where you dig.*

She picked up her clipboard, the weight of the pen suddenly feeling heavier in her hand. Ethan Wilde was more than a patient, of that she was certain. But whether he was an ally or a threat remained a question she couldn't yet answer.

For now, she turned her attention back to the charts, her resolve hardening. Whatever Ethan was hiding, she would find out. And if he was right about one thing, it was that something in this hospital wasn't as it seemed.

Chapter 4
Unspoken Warnings

The sterile light of the hospital computer screen illuminated Lily's face as she sat in the corner of the staff lounge, flipping through patient records with a tight knot in her stomach. Every click of the mouse felt like a betrayal, the weight of her decision pressing heavier with each name she scrolled past.

A shadow moved behind her. She turned quickly, her nerves on edge, only to find Ethan standing there, his arms crossed, his gaze steady.

"Didn't mean to startle you," he said softly, though the sharpness in his tone betrayed his impatience.

"You didn't," she replied tersely, turning back to the screen. "But you shouldn't be here. If anyone sees you—"

"They won't," Ethan interrupted, stepping closer. "I know how to stay invisible. Have you found anything?"

Lily shot him a sharp look. "You mean, have I risked my career enough for you yet? Not quite."

He held her gaze, his expression unreadable. "You agreed to this, Lily. We don't have time to second-guess every step."

Her fingers hovered over the keyboard as she exhaled slowly. "I didn't agree to becoming your lackey, Ethan. I'm doing this because it's the only way I can protect my patients."

"And I'm doing this to protect a hell of a lot more than just your patients," he said evenly. "We're on the same side, even if it doesn't feel that way right now."

She hesitated, her defenses prickling at his calm certainty. "You talk like you have all the answers, like you're the only one who knows what's really at stake. But you're not the one risking everything, Ethan. I am."

His jaw tightened, and he leaned in, lowering his voice. "You think I'm not risking anything? Every day I spend here, I'm one step closer to being exposed. If that happens, this entire operation falls apart. And if you think that doesn't keep me up at night, you're wrong."

The intensity in his eyes made her pause, her fingers still hovering over the keyboard. She hated that he was right, hated that he always seemed so sure of himself. But most of all, she hated that his conviction was starting to chip away at her own walls.

"Fine," she said finally, breaking the tension as she turned back to the screen. "But you'd better make this worth it."

"I will," he replied, his voice steady but quieter now. "What have you found so far?"

She clicked through another set of files, her tone clipped. "Two patients with matching symptoms had unusual notations in their charts—labs that were repeated for no clear reason, additional tests ordered that no one ever followed up on. It's sloppy, but it's there."

Ethan nodded, leaning closer to get a better look. "Who ordered the tests?"

She hesitated, scrolling back to the notes. "Dr. Robbins and Dr. Vega. Both attending physicians. But Vega's the one whose name shows up more consistently."

"Do you trust her?" Ethan asked, his voice sharp.

"I trust her to be thorough," Lily replied carefully. "She's not the type to leave loose ends, which makes this even more unusual."

Ethan straightened, his expression darkening. "Then she might not be as clean as you think."

"You don't know that," Lily snapped, a protective edge in her voice. "And I'm not about to accuse someone without proof."

"I'm not asking you to," he said, his tone softening just a fraction. "But we can't ignore patterns. If her name keeps coming up, we have to follow it."

Lily sighed, leaning back in her chair and rubbing her temples. "This is why I didn't want to get involved. I hate this. I hate doubting people I work with."

"Believe me," Ethan said, his voice quieter now, "I know how that feels."

She glanced at him, her irritation fading slightly at the vulnerability in his tone. "You don't seem like the type to doubt anyone. Or anything."

"Then you don't know me as well as you think," he replied, his gaze meeting hers. "This job forces you to question everything. Everyone. It's not something you get used to—it's something you survive."

His words hung in the air, heavier than she wanted to admit. She looked back at the screen, her resolve hardening. "Survive. Right. Well, if you're expecting me to help you tear apart my entire world, don't think for a second I'll do it quietly."

A faint smile tugged at the corner of his mouth. "I wouldn't expect anything less."

She scoffed, shaking her head as she clicked through another file. "You're impossible, you know that?"

"So I've been told," he replied, stepping back toward the shadows. "Keep digging. Let me know what you find."

"And what about you?" she asked, glancing at him over her shoulder. "What exactly are you doing while I'm risking everything here?"

"Following another lead," he said simply. "But I'll be close if you need me."

"Of course you will," she muttered, returning her focus to the screen. "Because why make this easy?"

He didn't respond, but she felt his gaze linger a moment longer before he slipped out of the room as quietly as he'd arrived.

Lily sighed, staring at the screen, her thoughts spinning. Their partnership was fragile at best, built on a foundation of mistrust and necessity. And yet, as much as she hated it, a part of her couldn't deny that Ethan's presence—his persistence—was starting to get under her skin.

Lily stood outside the patient's room, the chart clutched in her hands. The hallway buzzed with the usual controlled chaos of the ER, but all she could focus on was the name at the top of the file: Margaret Fields. A sixty-two-year-old woman admitted with fever, lethargy, and a persistent cough that had baffled the attending staff. No amount of fluids or standard respiratory treatments seemed to touch it.

Ethan stood beside her, his arms crossed, his expression unreadable but alert. He scanned the surroundings as if expecting someone to swoop in and stop them at any moment.

"Are you sure about this?" she asked, her voice low. "If anyone asks why you're here…"

"I'll disappear," Ethan interrupted, his tone calm but firm. "But they won't ask. Let's go."

Lily exhaled slowly and pushed the door open, stepping inside. Margaret lay on the bed, her gray hair matted to her forehead with sweat. She looked up weakly as they entered, her breath rattling with each inhale.

“Mrs. Fields,” Lily said gently, moving to the bedside. “I’m Dr. Chen. How are you feeling?”

“Like I’ve been hit by a truck,” Margaret rasped, attempting a weak smile. “And then it backed up for good measure.”

Lily chuckled softly, glancing at Ethan as he hung back near the door. “We’re going to take a closer look, alright? See if we can figure out what’s going on.”

Margaret nodded faintly, her eyelids heavy. “That’d be nice. I don’t… I don’t have much left in the tank.”

As Lily adjusted Margaret’s oxygen mask and checked her vitals, Ethan moved to the corner of the room, his eyes scanning the monitors and equipment. He leaned slightly toward Lily, his voice low and quiet.

“Her oxygen saturation is dropping,” he noted. “Eighty-five percent. That’s low for someone already on support.”

Lily nodded, her tone professional. “Her symptoms aren’t responding to standard treatments. The antibiotics we’ve tried? No effect. Steroids? Same story.”

“And the labs?” Ethan asked.

"Elevated white blood cell count, but no obvious bacterial source," Lily replied, her voice tightening with frustration. "It's like her body's fighting something we can't pinpoint."

Margaret stirred, her voice faint but clear enough to cut through the air. "It's getting worse, isn't it? I can feel it."

Lily leaned closer, her voice softening. "We're doing everything we can to figure this out, Mrs. Fields. I promise."

Margaret's lips quirked into a tired smile. "You're kind, Doc. But I've been around long enough to know when the chips aren't in my favor."

Lily felt a pang of guilt, glancing briefly at Ethan before returning her focus to her patient. "We're not giving up. Neither should you."

Margaret closed her eyes, her breathing slow and shallow, as though the effort of speaking had drained her completely. Lily stepped away from the bed, signaling Ethan to follow her to the far side of the room.

"She doesn't have much time," she said quietly, the frustration clear in her tone. "And we're no closer to figuring out what's causing this."

Ethan's gaze shifted from the patient to Lily, his voice steady. "This fits the pattern. Fever, respiratory distress, extreme fatigue—all signs of a targeted pathogen."

Lily frowned, crossing her arms. "It still doesn't make sense. If this is the work of your 'operative,' why target someone like her? She's not connected to anything high-profile."

"Testing," Ethan replied grimly. "She's a test subject. Random patients, no discernible connection, to keep it under the radar."

Lily's stomach turned at the thought. "You're saying they're experimenting on her. Like she's… disposable?"

Ethan nodded, his face hard. "Exactly. And if we don't act fast, she won't be the last."

The weight of his words settled heavily on her shoulders. She glanced back at Margaret, her frail figure a stark reminder of the stakes they were playing with. "So what do we do?" she asked, her voice quiet but determined. "How do we stop this?"

"We start here," Ethan said, his tone firm. "Her labs, her symptoms—they're clues. If we can trace them to the source, we might find a way to stop this before it spreads."

Lily hesitated, her medical training clashing with the risk Ethan's plan demanded. But when she looked at Margaret, the decision became painfully clear. "I'll pull the full workup," she said finally. "There has to be something we're missing."

Ethan's expression softened slightly, a glimmer of gratitude breaking through his usual guarded demeanor. "Thank you, Lily. I know this isn't easy."

"No," she replied, her voice tinged with frustration. "It's not. But if this is the only way to save her, then I don't have a choice."

She turned back to Margaret, adjusting her blanket and brushing a strand of hair from her face. "Hang in there, Mrs. Fields. We're going to get to the bottom of this."

Margaret stirred, her lips forming a faint smile. "I believe you, Doc."

As Lily and Ethan left the room, the tension between them remained thick, but there was a sense of unspoken understanding growing. They were in this together now, bound by a shared determination—and a responsibility neither could ignore.

Lily leaned against the counter in the empty staff lounge, her arms crossed as she watched Ethan pace near the window. The city lights cast fractured reflections against the glass, adding a surreal edge to the conversation they were about to have.

"You've been quiet," she said, her voice breaking the charged silence.

Ethan stopped, turning to face her with a rueful smile. "You have that effect on people."

"Not what I meant," she replied, her tone softening. "Back there, with Margaret… you seemed shaken."

His smile faded, replaced by a far-off look that tugged at something inside her. "It's hard to watch," he admitted, his voice low. "People suffering, knowing someone pulled the strings to put them there."

Lily's brow furrowed as she studied him, the quiet intensity in his tone cutting through her defenses. "You've seen this before, haven't you? This kind of calculated destruction."

Ethan let out a hollow laugh, leaning against the window frame. "You could say that. My job… it's not just about stopping threats. It's about seeing the worst people are capable of and trying to stop it before it spreads."

She tilted her head, curiosity mingling with a growing unease. "And how did you end up with that job? Seems like a far cry from… whatever else you could've been doing."

He hesitated, his gaze dropping to the floor. For a moment, she thought he wouldn't answer, but then he straightened, his voice steady. "I was good at reading people. Spotting patterns. The kind of skills that get noticed when the military is looking for specialists."

"Specialists?" she repeated, her tone laced with skepticism. "You make it sound so clinical."

"Because it is," he replied simply. "It has to be. You can't let it get personal."

Lily scoffed, shaking her head. "You're standing here in a hospital, watching innocent people suffer, and you're telling me it's not personal?"

He met her gaze then, his expression hard. "It's not that simple. If you let it become personal, you start making mistakes. You hesitate when you can't afford to."

Her arms fell to her sides, her voice softening. "But you feel it, don't you? The weight of it. Otherwise, you wouldn't be here, putting yourself on the line."

His silence was answer enough, and for the first time, she saw a crack in the armor he wore so carefully. When he finally spoke, his voice was quieter, tinged with something she couldn't quite name.

"I've seen what happens when we fail," he said, his eyes distant. "It's not just about numbers or casualties. It's about the lives you can't save because you weren't fast enough, smart enough, good enough."

Lily felt a lump form in her throat, the raw honesty in his words cutting through her. "You carry that with you."

He nodded, his expression softening. "Every day."

The room fell into a heavy silence, broken only by the hum of the refrigerator in the corner. She crossed the distance between them, her voice gentler now. "And now? Are you worried this will be one of those times?"

Ethan looked at her, the vulnerability in his gaze startling her. "I'm always worried, Lily. But that's why we have to keep moving. If we stop, even for a second, we lose."

She swallowed hard, the weight of his words settling over her. "You're not alone in this," she said quietly. "Whatever happens, we're in it together."

He tilted his head, a faint smile tugging at the corner of his lips. "That sounds dangerously like trust."

"Maybe it is," she replied, surprising herself with the honesty in her tone.

For a moment, the tension between them shifted, softened. The roles they'd so carefully kept separate—doctor and patient, investigator and civilian—blurred under the weight of their shared burden. Lily felt the walls she'd built around herself beginning to crack, the connection between them pulling her closer than she'd intended.

"I'll take care of Margaret's labs," she said, breaking the silence but not the connection. "If there's a lead there, we'll find it."

"I know you will," Ethan replied, his voice steady again but still carrying a thread of warmth. "You're a lot stronger than you give yourself credit for, you know."

She smirked, shaking her head. "Don't get sappy on me now, Wilde."

"Wouldn't dream of it," he said, the familiar glint of mischief returning to his eyes. But as he stepped back, the weight of the moment lingered, an unspoken promise hanging between them.

As Lily turned to leave the lounge, her mind was a swirl of emotions—doubt, fear, and something else she wasn't ready to name. Whatever this was, whatever danger lay ahead, one thing was certain: she and Ethan were bound now, by a secret and a threat that would test them both in ways neither could predict.

The glow of the computer screen was the only light in the room, casting pale blue shadows across the walls. The hospital had finally quieted, the hum of machines and distant murmur of voices reduced to a low background rhythm. Lily sat hunched over the desk in the corner of the staff lounge, a stack of patient files beside her. Her eyes burned from staring at the screen too long, but the adrenaline coursing through her veins kept her alert.

Ethan sat across from her, leaning back in his chair, his arms crossed as he watched her work. He had been quiet for most of the night, letting her sort through the data in her own way. It was a dynamic she hadn't expected—he, the interloper, letting her lead. It felt oddly natural.

"This is the third one," Lily muttered, breaking the silence as she pulled up another file. "Elevated white blood cell count, respiratory distress, fatigue. The same unexplained lethargy. It's like clockwork."

Ethan straightened, his focus narrowing as he leaned closer. "And the attending notes?"

"Minimal," she replied, frustration tightening her voice. "They treated the symptoms, but no one thought to connect the dots. It's like no one wanted to see the pattern."

"Or someone made sure they didn't," Ethan said grimly.

The thought sent a chill through her, but she nodded, her fingers flying across the keyboard. "Margaret's labs match this one, and the guy from last week—Casey Thompson. Both were admitted through the ER, treated for symptoms, and discharged without a clear diagnosis."

Ethan exhaled sharply, the weight of confirmation settling between them. "That's three cases too many."

Lily sat back, rubbing her temples as her mind raced. The web they were uncovering was more intricate than she'd imagined, its threads stretching further with each new discovery. "How far does this go, Ethan? How many more patients are we going to find?"

He didn't answer immediately, his gaze fixed on the monitor as though searching for something she couldn't see. When he finally spoke, his voice was quiet, steady. "It's hard to say. But every case we find brings us closer to the truth."

She looked at him then, her exhaustion momentarily forgotten. There was something in his tone—a resolve that felt unshakable. It wasn't the confidence of someone who enjoyed being in control. It was the determination of someone who had no choice but to keep going.

"Why do you do it?" she asked suddenly, her voice softer now. "This job, this life—it's not just about protecting people, is it?"

He glanced at her, his expression momentarily caught off guard. But then he smiled faintly, his shoulders relaxing just a fraction. "You're right. It's not just about protecting people. It's about making sure the ones who think they're untouchable know they're not."

The simplicity of his answer hit her harder than she expected, and for a moment, the room felt heavier. "It's lonely, isn't it?" she said, more to herself than to him.

"It can be," he admitted after a pause. "But moments like this? Knowing someone's willing to step into the chaos with you? That makes it easier."

She turned back to the monitor, her heart twisting at his words. There was a quiet sincerity in them that she wasn't prepared for, a vulnerability that made her chest ache. She didn't reply, letting the soft clicking of the keyboard fill the silence instead.

After a few minutes, Ethan's voice broke through the stillness. "Lily."

She looked up, startled by the way he said her name—softly, almost reverently. He wasn't looking at the monitor anymore. His gaze was fixed on her, steady and unflinching.

"Thank you," he said simply. "For trusting me. For not walking away."

Her throat tightened, and she swallowed hard, nodding. "Don't make me regret it."

His lips quirked into a faint smile. "I won't."

The air between them shifted, heavy with an unspoken understanding. It wasn't a grand moment, not something that would make headlines or shake the world. But to Lily, it felt monumental. In the midst of the uncertainty, the danger, the blurred lines of their roles, there was this—a bond forged not out of obligation, but out of a shared purpose.

As she turned back to the files, the exhaustion that had weighed her down earlier seemed lighter. The stakes were higher than she'd ever imagined, and the risks loomed large, but for the first time in a long time, she felt alive.

Ethan leaned back in his chair, his expression softening as he watched her. "We'll figure this out," he said quietly, as though it were a promise.

She didn't look up, but she nodded, a small smile tugging at her lips. "We'd better."

And for that moment, in the quiet stillness of the hospital night, it was enough.

Chapter 5
Trust and Betrayal

The ER was its usual symphony of noise and movement—monitors beeping, voices shouting orders, wheels of stretchers squeaking against the tile floor. But the sharp cry of "Code Blue! Room Three!" cut through the chaos like a siren.

Lily's heart jumped as she bolted toward the room, adrenaline pumping through her veins. Inside, the patient, an elderly man, lay motionless, his ashen face a stark contrast to the frantic activity around him.

"Nurse!" Lily barked. "Get the crash cart!"

"I'm on it!" Nina's voice rang back as she dashed to retrieve the cart.

Lily moved to the bedside, her hands trembling slightly as she checked for a pulse. Nothing. "Starting compressions," she announced, climbing onto the stool to begin CPR. The patient's chest sank beneath her hands, the rhythmic pressure a lifeline in the storm.

"Here!" Nina slid the crash cart into the room, her hands already moving to set up the defibrillator.

Lily barely had time to register someone else entering the room—a figure moving swiftly to her side. "Need a hand, Doc?"

The voice was calm, steady, and unmistakable.

"Ethan?" she blurted, her focus faltering for a split second.

"Focus," he said sharply, his tone snapping her back to the present.

She didn't have time to question him as he reached for the defibrillator pads, his movements precise and confident.

"You're not supposed to be here," Lily said, her voice strained as she continued compressions.

"And he's not supposed to be dying," Ethan replied without missing a beat. "What's the rhythm?"

Nina glanced at the monitor, her voice tight. "V-fib."

"Charging to 200 joules," Ethan announced, his hands working deftly. "Everyone clear."

The room froze for a heartbeat. Lily stepped back, her breath hitching as the defibrillator whined to life.

"Clear!" Ethan called, pressing the paddles to the patient's chest. The man's body jerked violently, then fell still.

Lily rushed forward, her eyes glued to the monitor. The chaotic peaks of ventricular fibrillation continued, unyielding.

"Resume compressions," Ethan ordered, his voice cutting through the tension like a scalpel.

Lily didn't hesitate. She moved back into position, her hands finding the rhythm again. "You know a lot for someone who's just a patient," she muttered, her words punctuated by each push of her palms.

"Long story," Ethan replied, his tone clipped as he recalibrated the machine. "Charging to 300. Clear!"

Again, the room stilled as the defibrillator delivered its charge. This time, the monitor flickered, the jagged peaks of chaos shifting into the steady rhythm of a heartbeat.

"We've got a pulse," Nina confirmed, her voice breaking the fragile silence.

Lily exhaled shakily, stepping back from the bed. Sweat clung to her forehead, and her arms ached from the effort, but the sight of the patient's chest rising and falling was enough to steady her nerves.

"Good work, team," she said, her voice quieter now as she turned to Nina. "Let's stabilize him and get him to the ICU."

As the nurses moved to secure the patient's lines and monitors, Lily turned to Ethan, who stood calmly by the crash cart, as if saving a life was just another part of his day.

"You shouldn't have been in here," she said, her tone sharp but wavering with exhaustion. "And yet, I couldn't have done that without you."

Ethan's lips curved into a faint smile, his posture relaxed. "I figured you could use the help."

"That's not the point," Lily snapped, her frustration bubbling to the surface. "You knew exactly what to do. That wasn't just instinct. Who are you, really?"

He held her gaze for a moment, the smirk fading from his face. "Just someone who's been in a few tight spots," he said cryptically.

"That's not an answer," she countered, stepping closer.

"It's the only one you're getting," Ethan replied, his tone soft but resolute. He glanced at the patient, then back at her. "You're good at what you do, Doc. Keep it up."

Before Lily could press him further, Ethan turned and walked out of the room, leaving her standing there, her mind racing.

She watched his retreating figure, her pulse still racing from the adrenaline, and a new thought gnawed at her. Ethan Wilde wasn't just a patient, and this wasn't just a chance encounter.

Something about him didn't fit.

And for the first time, she wasn't sure if that was a good thing—or a very dangerous one.

Lily found him leaning against a shadowed wall near the stairwell, a coffee cup balanced precariously on the railing. The hum of the hospital felt distant here, muffled by the heavy door that separated this corner from the rest of the ER. Ethan didn't look up as she approached, but his posture stiffened slightly, as if he'd been expecting her.

"Ethan," she said, her voice sharp.

He glanced up, his expression calm but guarded. "Doc," he greeted casually, taking a slow sip of his coffee.

Lily didn't bother with pleasantries. "We need to talk."

"Talking's free," he said, setting the cup down. "But I'm guessing this isn't a social visit."

"It's about the infections," she said bluntly, crossing her arms.

Ethan's smirk faltered, but only for a second. "What infections?"

"The ones spreading through the hospital," she said, her tone growing sharper. "The fever, the respiratory issues, the unexplained lab results—it's a pattern, and you know it."

"Do I?" Ethan replied, tilting his head.

"Don't play dumb with me," she snapped, stepping closer. "You've been watching me. Watching the patients. You knew something was off before anyone else did."

Ethan sighed, running a hand through his hair. "Lily—"

"No," she interrupted, her frustration bubbling over. "Don't try to deflect. You've been dropping hints, giving me cryptic warnings, acting like you're trying to help. But you're not telling me everything, and I need to know why."

For the first time, Ethan didn't meet her gaze. His jaw tightened, and he leaned back against the wall, his hands sliding into his pockets. "You don't want to go down this road," he said quietly.

"That's not your decision to make," she said, her voice steady but fierce. "If you know something, you owe it to these patients—to this hospital—to tell me."

Ethan looked at her then, his eyes dark and unreadable. "You're a good doctor, Lily. You care about your patients. I respect that."

"This isn't about me," she snapped. "This is about what's happening here. Are you involved?"

Silence hung between them, heavy and suffocating.

"Are you?" she pressed, stepping closer.

Ethan's lips tightened into a thin line. "You don't know what you're asking," he said finally, his voice low and steady.

"Then enlighten me," she shot back.

"It's not that simple," Ethan said, his tone shifting to something harder, almost defensive. "You think this is just about a few sick patients? You think I'm just some guy wandering around, sticking my nose where it doesn't belong?"

"That's exactly what I think," Lily said. "Unless you give me a reason to think otherwise."

Ethan pushed off the wall, closing the distance between them. His movements were calm, deliberate, but there was an intensity in his gaze that made her heart pound. "There are things happening here that you can't even begin to understand," he said. "Things that go way beyond this hospital. Beyond you. Beyond me."

"That's not an answer," she said, holding her ground.

"It's the only one I can give you right now," Ethan replied.

Lily's patience snapped. "Why are you even here, Ethan? You show up with your cracked rib and your smirks and your warnings, and now you're telling me this is bigger than I realize? What the hell are you hiding?"

Ethan exhaled sharply, stepping back. "I'm trying to protect you," he said finally.

"Protect me?" she repeated, incredulous. "From what?"

Ethan hesitated, his gaze flicking away for just a moment before locking back onto hers. "From finding answers you're not ready for," he said quietly.

Lily's breath caught in her throat, her frustration warring with a flicker of unease. "I'm not afraid of the truth, Ethan."

"Maybe you should be," he said.

His words hung in the air, heavy and unyielding. Lily searched his face for some crack in his armor, some hint of the vulnerability she'd glimpsed earlier, but it was gone.

"I can't help these patients if I don't know what's going on," she said, her voice softening but no less determined.

Ethan stared at her for a long moment before stepping back. "You'll find out soon enough," he said. "But when you do, don't say I didn't warn you."

With that, he turned and walked away, leaving Lily standing there, her heart pounding and her mind racing.

The infections, the patients, Ethan's cryptic warnings—they were all pieces of a puzzle she wasn't sure she wanted to solve. But one thing was clear: Ethan Wilde wasn't just a patient, and whatever he was hiding, it was bigger than she'd imagined.

The hospital's cafeteria was nearly empty in the late afternoon, the usual rush of staff and visitors having ebbed into a quiet lull. Lily sat at a small table by the window, staring into her untouched cup of coffee. She wasn't even sure why she was here—her thoughts were too tangled to focus on the patient charts she'd brought with her.

"Mind if I join you?"

The voice was familiar, smooth, and just a bit too confident. Lily looked up to see Ethan Wilde standing on the other side of the table, holding a coffee cup of his own.

"I'm working," she said flatly, though the charts in front of her told a different story.

"Sure you are," Ethan said, slipping into the chair across from her without waiting for permission.

Lily sighed, her frustration bubbling just below the surface. "What do you want, Ethan?"

"To talk," he said, leaning back in his chair. "You seem tense."

"Gee, I wonder why," she snapped, her eyes narrowing. "Maybe it has something to do with a certain someone who keeps dropping cryptic warnings instead of giving me real answers."

Ethan smirked, taking a slow sip of his coffee. "You're stubborn, I'll give you that."

"I'm persistent," she corrected. "And right now, I'm persistently trying to figure out what's going on with these infections. So unless you have something useful to say—"

"I might," he interrupted, his tone softening. "But it depends."

"Depends on what?"

"On whether you're ready to hear it."

Lily set her coffee cup down harder than she intended, the ceramic clinking sharply against the table. "I'm ready, Ethan. I've been ready since the first patient came in with these symptoms."

He studied her for a moment, his gaze searching her face as though trying to measure her resolve. "Alright," he said finally, leaning forward slightly. "Let's start small. What do you know about the infections so far?"

"They're not seasonal," she said immediately, her voice firm. "The symptoms are too severe, and the cases are clustering in a way that doesn't make sense for a normal outbreak. The labs aren't showing anything conclusive, but it feels… deliberate."

Ethan nodded slowly, a flicker of approval crossing his face. "Good. You're paying attention."

"Of course I am," she said, exasperated. "Now tell me what you know."

He hesitated, his fingers tapping lightly against his coffee cup. "Let's just say you're on the right track," he said cryptically.

Lily groaned, leaning back in her chair. "Unbelievable. You're doing it again."

"Doing what?"

"Speaking in riddles," she snapped. "Just say what you mean, Ethan!"

"Alright," he said quietly, his tone shifting. "I think someone's testing something. Something they shouldn't be."

Her breath caught, the weight of his words sinking in. "Testing… like a pathogen?"

He didn't answer immediately, but his silence spoke volumes.

"Ethan," she pressed, her voice low.

He sighed, running a hand through his hair. "I can't give you details, Doc. Not yet. But you're right—this isn't natural. And whoever's behind it? They don't care about the people getting sick."

Lily stared at him, her mind racing. "Why do you know this?"

He hesitated again, his gaze dropping to the table. "Because I've seen it before."

The vulnerability in his voice caught her off guard. She leaned forward, her tone softening. "Seen what?"

Ethan took a long sip of his coffee before answering. "Places like this. People like you, doing everything they can to save lives, while someone else pulls the strings in the background. I've been on the wrong side of it more than once."

His words were careful, deliberate, but there was an undercurrent of emotion that made her pause. For the first time, she saw something raw behind his sharp wit and easy charm—a glimpse of the man beneath the facade.

"Why didn't you say anything sooner?" she asked quietly.

"Would you have believed me?" he countered, his eyes meeting hers.

Lily didn't answer right away. She wanted to say yes, but she wasn't sure it would have been true.

Ethan leaned back, his smirk returning but softer this time. "You're not like anyone else here," he said, his voice lighter now. "Most people wouldn't even ask the questions you're asking."

She folded her arms, her expression skeptical but curious. "Flattery won't get you out of this, you know."

"It's not flattery," he said simply. "It's the truth."

Lily hesitated, then nodded slightly. "Alright," she said. "You've got my attention. But if you're going to keep hinting at things without giving me answers, this is going to get old fast."

Ethan's lips quirked into a faint smile. "Fair enough, Doc. I'll try to be a little less cryptic."

As he stood to leave, Lily felt a strange mix of frustration and intrigue. Ethan Wilde was still an enigma, but for the first time, she felt like she'd seen a crack in his armor—a moment of honesty that made her believe he might be more than just trouble.

"You're not like anyone else here," she admitted softly, more to herself than to him.

Ethan glanced back, his smirk widening. "Neither are you, Lily."

And with that, he was gone, leaving her with more questions than answers—and a growing sense that she couldn't turn back now.

The dimly lit storage room was quiet, save for the hum of the overhead fluorescent light. Lily leaned against the stainless steel counter, her arms crossed and her expression skeptical. Ethan stood a few feet away, his hands resting casually on the back of a chair, his demeanor calm but his eyes carrying a weight she couldn't ignore.

"This isn't just about a virus, is it?" Lily broke the silence, her voice steady but laced with frustration. "You've been dodging my questions since day one, Ethan. I need answers."

Ethan sighed, rubbing the back of his neck as if trying to buy time. "You're right. It's not just about the virus."

"Then what is it about?" she pressed, her patience wearing thin.

He glanced at her, his expression unreadable. "Have you ever heard the phrase 'controlled chaos'?"

Lily frowned. "What are you talking about?"

"That's what's happening here," Ethan said, his tone measured. "This outbreak—it's not an accident. Someone's orchestrating it, testing something they don't want anyone to know about."

Her breath caught, the weight of his words sinking in. "Testing what?"

"A pathogen," he said bluntly.

Lily's chest tightened. "That's insane. You're saying someone's deliberately infecting people?"

"Exactly," Ethan said, his voice low but firm.

She shook her head, pacing the small room. "This is a hospital, Ethan. It's supposed to be a place where people get better, not where they're used as guinea pigs."

"You think I don't know that?" he shot back, his calm exterior cracking. "I've seen it before, Lily. Places just like this, where people come in for help and end up as part of someone else's experiment."

Lily stopped pacing, her arms falling to her sides. "If you've seen this before, why didn't you stop it?"

Ethan hesitated, his jaw tightening. "Because last time, I didn't know what I was walking into until it was too late. I wasn't prepared. But this time…"

"This time, what?" she prompted.

"This time, I'm not alone," Ethan said, his gaze locking with hers.

The words hung in the air, heavy and unspoken. For the first time, Lily saw something in him she hadn't noticed before—vulnerability, yes, but also determination. He wasn't just warning her anymore. He was asking her for help.

"You need me," she said, her voice soft but certain.

"I do," he admitted, his tone losing its usual edge. "You're the only one here who sees what's really happening. The others? They'd write me off as paranoid or worse. But you—you ask the right questions. You dig deeper. That's what we need right now."

Lily hesitated, her mind racing. "We?"

Ethan's lips curved into a faint, humorless smile. "You're in this now, Doc. Whether you like it or not."

She crossed her arms again, her skepticism returning. "And why should I trust you?"

"Because I don't have a choice," he said simply. "And neither do you."

The honesty in his voice caught her off guard. She studied him for a long moment, her instincts warring with her logic. Ethan Wilde was still a mystery, but if even half of what he was saying was true, she couldn't ignore it.

"What do you need from me?" she asked finally, her voice quiet.

Ethan straightened, his expression serious. "Access. Records. Patterns. You've already started connecting the dots, but I need your help to see the whole picture. If we're going to figure out who's behind this—and stop them—we need to work together."

Lily exhaled slowly, the weight of the decision pressing down on her. "If we do this, there's no turning back," she said.

"I know," Ethan said, his voice steady. "But this isn't just about the patients here, Lily. It's bigger than that. If we don't act, more people will get hurt."

Her resolve hardened. She stepped forward, her eyes meeting his. "Alright," she said. "I'm in. But if you hold anything back—anything—I'm done."

"Fair enough," Ethan said, offering a faint smile.

Lily extended her hand, and after a brief hesitation, he took it. His grip was firm, steady, and for the first time, she felt like they were on the same side.

"Let's get to work," she said.

Ethan nodded, a glimmer of relief flashing across his face. "We don't have much time."

As they left the room together, the uncertainty between them began to give way to a fragile alliance. For better or worse, they were in this together now.

Chapter 6
Threads in the Dark

Lily's fingers flew across the keyboard, the glow of the hospital's records database illuminating her tense features. Her heart pounded in her chest as she skimmed through the files, her pulse racing faster with each second that ticked by. She had slipped into an empty administrative office under the guise of reviewing routine reports, but the stakes were anything but ordinary.

"Come on," she muttered under her breath, her eyes scanning the entries for something—anything—that could connect the dots Ethan had uncovered. "Where are you…"

The sound of a door handle turning froze her in place. Panic surged through her veins as the door creaked open behind her.

"Dr. Chen," Dr. Harlow's voice cut through the silence like a blade. "What are you doing?"

Lily turned slowly, her expression carefully neutral, though her mind raced to come up with an excuse. Harlow stood in the doorway, his arms crossed, his sharp gaze locked onto her. The room felt smaller with him there, his presence suffocating.

"Dr. Harlow," she said, forcing a smile. "I was just reviewing patient histories. I noticed some inconsistencies in—"

"Inconsistencies?" he interrupted, stepping further into the room. His tone was calm, but his eyes gleamed with something darker. "And you thought it appropriate to dig through restricted files without authorization?"

Her throat tightened, but she held his gaze. "I wasn't digging. I just… wanted to ensure nothing was overlooked in the lab reports. Given the recent infections, I thought it was worth double-checking."

Harlow's lips pressed into a thin line as he moved to the desk, towering over her. "And what, exactly, are you hoping to find?"

"Connections," she replied, her voice steadier than she felt. "I've seen patterns that don't make sense, and I wanted to—"

"You wanted to play detective," he said sharply, cutting her off again. "That's not your role, Dr. Chen. Your job is to treat patients, not investigate imaginary conspiracies."

"They're not imaginary," she countered, her frustration breaking through. "Patients are dying, Dr. Harlow. We can't ignore that."

His eyes narrowed, and for a long moment, the only sound was the faint hum of the computer. "Careful," he said finally, his voice dropping to a menacing calm. "You're overstepping."

The intensity of his words sent a chill down her spine. She forced herself to stand, stepping out from behind the desk to face him directly. "I'm overstepping because no one else is asking these questions. If we don't figure out what's happening—"

"What's happening," he snapped, his voice rising, "is that you're jeopardizing this hospital's reputation with your baseless accusations."

Lily clenched her fists at her sides, willing herself to stay calm. "This isn't about reputation. It's about saving lives."

Harlow's gaze bore into hers, and for a moment, she thought she saw a flicker of something—fear? Guilt? Whatever it was, it vanished as quickly as it appeared.

"Consider this your final warning, Dr. Chen," he said, his voice cold. "Stay in your lane. Leave the labs and the investigations to those qualified to handle them."

"And if I don't?" she asked, the question slipping out before she could stop it.

Harlow's jaw tightened, his voice dropping to a near whisper. "Then you'll find yourself with no lane at all."

The weight of his words settled heavily in the air between them. She swallowed hard, her mind racing. He was testing her, she realized. Watching her. Waiting to see how far she'd push.

"I understand," she said finally, her voice carefully measured. "I'll focus on patient care."

Harlow nodded curtly, stepping back toward the door. "Good. Remember, Dr. Chen—curiosity can be a dangerous thing."

She forced a tight smile, watching as he left the room. The moment the door clicked shut, she exhaled shakily, her knees threatening to give way. The close call left her rattled, but also more certain than ever: Harlow was hiding something.

She quickly logged out of the system, her fingers trembling slightly as she gathered her things. As she stepped out into the hallway, her eyes darted around, her instincts heightened. The walls of the hospital suddenly felt like they were closing in, the sterile white halls holding secrets she wasn't sure she was ready to face.

But as she made her way toward the safety of the staff lounge, one thought burned brightly in her mind: she couldn't stop now. Whatever was happening, whatever Harlow was hiding, she was going to uncover the truth—even if it meant risking everything.

The rooftop was quiet, the city sprawling beneath Lily in a blur of distant lights and muted noise. She leaned against the edge of the low barrier, the cool breeze brushing against her skin. It was a rare respite from the suffocating tension of the hospital's sterile walls, but even here, her mind refused to settle.

The sound of footsteps broke her thoughts. She turned, her heart giving a startled jump as Ethan emerged from the shadows.

"Figured I'd find you here," he said, his voice softer than usual.

Lily sighed, turning back to the skyline. "Didn't know I was that predictable."

"You're not," he replied, coming to stand beside her. "Just… a lucky guess."

For a moment, neither of them spoke. The city's hum filled the silence between them, the weight of the day hanging heavy in the air. Finally, Ethan broke the quiet.

"You've been quiet since Harlow," he said, glancing at her. "You alright?"

Lily gave a humorless laugh, shaking her head. "Define 'alright.' Because if it means feeling like the walls are closing in and the people I thought I could trust are lying to me, then yeah—I'm great."

Ethan leaned against the barrier, his expression unreadable. "You're not wrong to feel that way. Harlow's warning wasn't just a slap on the wrist—it was a message."

She frowned, her frustration bubbling to the surface. "And what am I supposed to do with that message? Back off? Pretend I don't see what's right in front of me?"

He met her gaze, his voice steady. "No. You keep going. But you do it carefully."

"Carefully," she repeated, her tone laced with bitterness. "Carefully doesn't seem to matter much when people like him have all the power."

Ethan's jaw tightened, his hands gripping the edge of the barrier. "Power like that doesn't last forever. It only holds as long as people let it."

Lily turned to him, studying his profile in the dim light. For the first time, she noticed how tired he looked—the lines around his eyes, the shadows that seemed etched into his face. "You talk like someone who's fought this battle before."

He hesitated, his gaze fixed on the horizon. "I have. Too many times."

The vulnerability in his voice caught her off guard, and she tilted her head, curiosity mingling with concern. "Ethan…"

"I wasn't always this person," he said, his voice quieter now. "The one who lives in the shadows, looking over his shoulder every second of the day. There was a time when I believed in… simpler things. Straightforward battles. Good versus evil."

"What changed?" she asked softly.

He let out a slow breath, his eyes darkening as he spoke. "I was part of an op a few years back. Routine mission—at least, that's what they told us. But things went wrong. People I trusted made choices I couldn't understand. Choices that cost lives."

Lily's chest tightened, the rawness in his tone stirring something in her. "I'm sorry."

He shook his head, his lips curving into a bitter smile. "I don't need sympathy, Lily. That's not why I'm telling you this. I'm telling you because… this, what we're dealing with now? It feels the same. Like the people pulling the strings don't care about the fallout, as long as they get what they want."

She looked down, her fingers curling around the edge of the barrier. "And what about you? Why are you still fighting, if it's cost you so much?"

He was quiet for a moment, his gaze distant. "Because someone has to. And because… I've seen what happens when no one does."

His words hung in the air, heavy with unspoken pain. Lily found herself wanting to reach out, to say something that might ease the weight he carried. But before she could, he turned to her, his expression softening.

"You've got that look," he said, a faint smile tugging at the corner of his lips. "Like you want to fix everything."

She raised an eyebrow, her tone dry. "And what's wrong with that?"

"Nothing," he admitted, his smile fading into something more sincere. "It's one of the things I like about you."

Her breath caught, her pulse skipping at the unexpected admission. She looked away quickly, her voice quieter now. "You don't even know me."

"I know enough," he said simply. "Enough to see that you care. That you're willing to fight, even when it scares you."

She swallowed hard, the truth in his words cutting deeper than she expected. "Maybe. Or maybe I'm just too stubborn to quit."

"Either way," he said, his voice steady, "it's what makes you dangerous—to people like Harlow. And it's what's going to get us through this."

She turned to him, her eyes meeting his. For a moment, the tension between them shifted, softened into something she couldn't quite name. The guarded walls he always kept up were down now, even if only for a moment, and she felt a strange pull toward him.

"Ethan," she said quietly, her voice almost a whisper.

"Yeah?" he replied, his gaze unwavering.

"Thanks," she said, surprising herself with the sincerity in her tone. "For… letting me in. Even just a little."

He nodded, a faint smile flickering across his face. "Don't get used to it."

She laughed softly, the sound breaking through the weight of the moment. As they stood there, the city stretching out beneath them, Lily realized she didn't just want to know more about Ethan—she needed to. And for the first time, the fear she'd been carrying felt just a little lighter.

The hospital conference room was dark, illuminated only by the glow of Lily's laptop screen. She sat at the long table, scrolling through patient records with laser focus. Ethan stood behind her, leaning over her shoulder, his presence steady but charged. The tension between them had grown inescapable, a mix of urgency and something neither of them dared to name.

"Look at this," Lily said, pointing to a cluster of highlighted notes on her screen. "Three patients admitted within a week of each other, all presenting with the same symptoms—fever, respiratory distress, and that extreme lethargy."

Ethan leaned closer, his brow furrowing as he read over her shoulder. "And all three discharged without a definitive diagnosis. They just labeled it as viral syndrome and moved on?"

She nodded, frustration lacing her voice. "Exactly. But here's what doesn't make sense: two of them were discharged in stable condition, but the third—Margaret Fields—was readmitted three days later in critical condition."

"Margaret's the one who flagged this whole thing for you," Ethan said, stepping back and crossing his arms. "So what's the connection between her and the other two?"

"That's the problem," Lily replied, her tone sharper than she intended. "I can't find one. Different attending physicians, different wings of the hospital, no overlapping visitors or medical histories. It's like someone went out of their way to keep these cases from linking up."

Ethan frowned, his jaw tightening. "Or they didn't think anyone would bother to look."

Lily turned in her chair to face him, her expression a mix of determination and frustration. "You think Harlow's behind this, don't you?"

Ethan's gaze was steady, though his voice softened. "I think he's part of it. Whether he's pulling the strings or just following orders, he knows more than he's letting on."

She shook her head, her voice tinged with disbelief. "I keep trying to wrap my head around it. Harlow's been here for decades. He's respected, trusted. How could someone like that…?"

"It's the perfect cover," Ethan said, cutting her off gently. "No one questions the guy who's spent his life saving people. That's how they get away with it."

Lily looked down at her hands, the weight of his words pressing down on her. "You talk about it like it's inevitable. Like people will always find ways to twist something good into something terrible."

"Not always," Ethan said, his voice softer now. "But often enough that you learn to see the signs."

She glanced up at him, her eyes searching his face. "And what about us? What do we do with what we're seeing?"

"We keep going," he replied firmly. "We dig until we have enough to expose them. Enough to shut this down."

Her lips pressed into a thin line, a mix of fear and resolve flickering in her eyes. "And if we don't find enough?"

Ethan leaned forward, his hands braced on the table as he locked eyes with her. "We will. You're too stubborn to let this go, and I'm too good at my job to fail."

She let out a small, incredulous laugh, shaking her head. "That's a hell of a pep talk, Wilde."

He smiled faintly, his tone softening. "It's the truth."

Their eyes met, the space between them charged with something unspoken. For a moment, the world outside the room seemed to fade, leaving only the quiet hum of the laptop and the intensity of their shared resolve. Lily felt her heart skip, the flicker of something warmer slipping through the cracks of her fear.

"I'll take it," she said finally, breaking the moment but not the connection.

Ethan straightened, gesturing toward the screen. "So what's next? Any other cases that fit the pattern?"

She nodded, turning back to the laptop and clicking through another set of files. "I pulled a list of recent patients who were readmitted within a week of being discharged. Four more with similar symptoms, and one of them… here.” She stopped, her voice catching. “It’s another case signed off by Harlow.”

Ethan’s jaw clenched, his voice darkening. “That’s not a coincidence.”

“No,” she agreed, her voice steady despite the dread creeping in. “It’s not.”

They worked in silence for a few minutes, the tension between them growing with every discovery. Each file, each overlooked symptom, painted a clearer picture of the web they were unraveling—and the danger that came with it.

Finally, Lily sat back, rubbing her temples. “This is bigger than I thought. It’s not just Harlow. It’s the entire system. Someone’s manipulating the protocols, hiding behind the hospital’s bureaucracy.”

“And that’s exactly how they’ve stayed hidden,” Ethan said, his voice grim. “But they didn’t count on you.”

She glanced at him, her lips curving into a faint smile. “Us. They didn’t count on us.”

Ethan paused, his expression softening as he met her gaze. “You’re right. Us.”

The word hung in the air, heavy with meaning. For a moment, the walls they’d both carefully built seemed to lower just enough for the truth to slip through: they weren’t just allies in this fight. They were something more, something neither of them dared to name yet.

"Alright," Lily said, turning back to the screen and breaking the spell. "Let's focus. We're not done yet."

Ethan nodded, his voice steady but warm. "Not even close."

And as they dove back into the files, the unspoken connection between them lingered—a quiet reminder that, no matter how dangerous the road ahead, they weren't facing it alone.

The conference room felt even quieter now, the hours stretching long into the night. The hospital buzzed faintly beyond the door, but inside, it was just Lily and Ethan, the glow of the laptop reflecting off their tense faces. The files lay scattered on the table between them—evidence of a conspiracy that was no longer theoretical.

Lily leaned back in her chair, exhaling sharply as she rubbed her temples. "This is insane," she murmured. "I don't even know how we got here."

Ethan, seated across from her, tilted his head slightly, his expression calm but intense. "You followed the truth. That's how."

She looked up at him, her brow furrowed. "And where has it gotten us? Into something so big, so dangerous, I can't even see the edges of it."

Ethan leaned forward, his hands clasped on the table. "That's what they want, Lily—for you to feel small, overwhelmed. That's how they win."

His words struck something deep inside her, and she straightened, her lips pressing into a determined line. "I hate that. I hate that they think they can just… get away with it. That no one will care enough to stop them."

"They're wrong," Ethan said, his voice steady. "We care. And that's enough."

"Is it?" she challenged, her voice sharp with frustration. "We're two people going up against—what? A network? An entire system? How do we even begin to fight something like that?"

Ethan's gaze didn't waver, his calm a stark contrast to her agitation. "We've already begun. Every file we've uncovered, every connection we've made—that's how it starts. Piece by piece."

Lily stared at him, her chest tightening. "And what happens when they find out? When they come after us?"

"They will," Ethan said simply, his tone carrying no fear, only certainty. "But when they do, we'll be ready."

The quiet confidence in his voice steadied her, and she nodded slowly, a flicker of resolve breaking through her doubt. "You really believe that, don't you?"

"I do," he replied, his eyes meeting hers. "Because I've seen what happens when people like them think no one's watching. And I've seen what happens when someone decides to stand up and fight."

She leaned forward, her voice soft but laced with fierce determination. "Then I'm in. All the way. Whatever it takes."

His expression softened, the corners of his mouth curving into the faintest hint of a smile. "Are you sure?"

"Ethan," she said firmly, holding his gaze. "People are dying. Patients I've treated—people I promised to help. If I don't do this, if I don't try to stop it, I'll never forgive myself. So yeah, I'm sure."

For a moment, the weight of her words hung between them, unspoken but palpable. Ethan nodded once, a quiet acknowledgment that carried more weight than any verbal promise. It was a shared understanding, a bond forged in the fire of their shared mission.

"You're not alone in this," he said softly, his voice carrying an unshakable conviction. "Whatever happens, we face it together."

Her throat tightened, and she nodded, her voice quieter now. "Together."

The room fell into silence again, but it wasn't empty. The scattered files, the dim light, the steady resolve in their eyes—

it all spoke of a commitment that neither of them could walk away from now.

After a moment, Lily broke the silence, her tone shifting to something lighter, almost teasing. "So, does this mean I get to boss you around now? Since we're partners and all."

Ethan chuckled, leaning back in his chair. "Depends. Are you good at giving orders?"

"I'm a doctor," she shot back, her lips curving into a faint smile. "Giving orders is half the job."

He smirked, shaking his head. "Alright, Doc. Let's see what you've got."

Her smile lingered as she turned back to the files, her fingers moving across the keyboard with renewed focus. The fear that had gripped her earlier was still there, but it had shifted—transformed into something sharper, something that fueled her determination rather than holding her back.

Ethan watched her work, his expression thoughtful. "You're different, you know."

She paused, glancing at him out of the corner of her eye. "Different how?"

"Most people would've walked away by now," he said, his tone sincere. "You didn't."

"Neither did you," she replied, her voice quiet but firm. "Maybe that's why we make a good team."

His smile was faint but genuine. "Maybe."

As they returned to their work, the night stretched on, but the weight of what lay ahead felt just a little lighter. They weren't just fighting for the truth anymore—they were fighting for each other, and that made all the difference.

Chapter 7
The Tipping Scales

The corridor was eerily silent, a stark contrast to the usual hum of activity in the hospital. Lily clutched the flashlight tighter, her breath shallow as she followed Ethan down the deserted hallway. The dim emergency lights cast long shadows on the walls, amplifying the uneasy stillness.

"This doesn't feel like the hospital anymore," she muttered, her voice barely above a whisper.

"It's not," Ethan replied without looking back. His tone was clipped, focused. "They've carved out a section just for this. Keep an eye out."

Lily's stomach churned as they approached an unmarked door at the end of the hall. It looked innocuous enough, but the faint, sterile hum that seeped from behind it told a different story. Ethan paused, glancing over his shoulder at her.

"You ready for this?" he asked, his voice softer now.

"Not even a little," she admitted, gripping the flashlight so tightly her knuckles turned white. "But I'm here."

He nodded, his expression unreadable, and pushed the door open.

The room beyond was a chilling vision of modern sterility and precision. Bright fluorescent lights buzzed overhead, illuminating rows of equipment Lily had only seen in high-level research labs. Stainless steel countertops gleamed, and racks of neatly labeled vials lined the walls. Monitors displayed streams of data she couldn't begin to decipher, the screens flickering with graphs and codes.

Lily's breath hitched as she stepped inside, the enormity of what she was seeing crashing over her. "This… this can't be here," she murmured. "This is a hospital, not a research facility."

"It's both," Ethan said grimly, moving toward one of the counters. He picked up a file folder, flipping through its contents. His jaw tightened. "This is where they're testing it."

She moved closer, her heart pounding as she scanned the labels on the vials. "Pathogen variants… bio-markers… immune suppression analysis?" Her voice grew shaky. "They're not just testing it. They're refining it."

Ethan placed the folder down, his eyes dark with anger. "They're building a weapon, Lily. A pathogen that can spread quietly and efficiently, targeting specific populations before anyone realizes what's happening."

Her knees threatened to buckle, and she gripped the counter for support. "And they're doing it here, in a hospital. Using patients as guinea pigs."

Ethan turned to her, his expression softening just enough to show his concern. "This is why we're here. To stop this."

Lily's gaze darted around the room, landing on a small cage in the corner containing several white mice. They moved sluggishly, their breathing labored. "They're sick," she said, her voice barely above a whisper. "They're testing the effects before moving to humans."

Ethan followed her gaze, his jaw tightening further. "And the patients—they're the next phase."

A wave of nausea rolled over her, and she pressed a hand to her mouth. "This is… monstrous. Who could do something like this?"

"The same kind of people who think lives are expendable," Ethan said, his voice cold. "People like Harlow."

Lily turned to him, her eyes wide. "You think he knows about this?"

Ethan nodded grimly. "He's not just involved—he's helping orchestrate it. This kind of setup requires coordination, funding, and someone on the inside who knows how to keep it under wraps."

Her chest tightened as the full scope of their discovery sank in. "This is bigger than I imagined. So much bigger."

Ethan moved closer, placing a steadying hand on her arm. "I know it's overwhelming, but we're not turning back now. This lab—this is the proof we need."

"But what do we do with it?" she asked, her voice trembling. "We can't just… expose this without evidence. They'll bury it. They'll bury us."

Ethan's grip on her arm tightened, his voice filled with quiet resolve. "Then we get more. We dig deeper, find the names, the connections. And when we move, we make sure they can't cover it up."

She stared at him, the fear in her chest mingling with a flicker of hope. "And what if they find us first?"

"They won't," he said firmly. "Not if we stay smart, stay ahead. This is just the beginning."

Lily looked back at the lab, the sterile hum of the machines filling her ears. The implications of their discovery settled heavily on her shoulders, but so did the realization that they were closer than ever to exposing the truth.

"Alright," she said, her voice steadier now. "But if we're going to do this, we do it right. No more close calls. No more guessing."

Ethan nodded, his expression softening just enough to reveal a trace of admiration. "You're stronger than you give yourself credit for, you know."

She shot him a faint smile, though it didn't reach her eyes. "Let's hope I don't have to prove it."

As they left the lab, the weight of what they had uncovered pressed heavily on them both. But for the first time, Lily felt her fear giving way to something sharper, more focused. Determination burned in her chest. They would stop this—no matter what it took.

Lily stood frozen, her gaze locked on the file in her hands. The room felt colder now, the hum of the hidden lab's machinery fading into the background as her eyes scanned the page. Each word she read chipped away at the foundation of trust she'd built over years of working under Dr. Harlow.

"No," she whispered, shaking her head. "This can't be right."

Ethan stepped closer, his gaze sharp as he peered over her shoulder. "What is it?"

She didn't answer immediately, her fingers trembling as she flipped to the next page. It was all there—test authorizations, lab results, signed orders. Every document bore the same unmistakable signature: Dr. Theodore Harlow.

"His name's on everything," she said finally, her voice trembling. "He's the one ordering the tests. Coordinating the labs. It's him."

Ethan took the file from her, his jaw tightening as he scanned the pages. "It's not just him," he said after a moment. "He's working with someone—there are references here to external funding, outside consultation. This is part of something bigger."

Lily turned away, her chest tightening as she struggled to process the betrayal. "But why? Why would he do this? He's a doctor, Ethan. He's supposed to save lives, not… not this."

Ethan set the file down, his voice steady but grim. "Sometimes it's about power. Or money. Or control. People like Harlow don't start out doing things like this—they get pulled in, little by little, until there's no turning back."

She spun around to face him, anger flashing in her eyes. "You're saying this like it's inevitable. Like it's just something that happens to people in his position."

"I'm saying it because I've seen it before," Ethan replied, his tone quiet but firm. "This isn't about who he used to be. It's about who he is now—and what he's willing to do to keep this going."

Lily shook her head, pacing the length of the lab. "I can't believe it. I trusted him. He was my mentor, Ethan. He taught me everything I know about medicine, about patient care. And now I find out he's been—what? Using this hospital as a testing ground for a bioweapon?"

"Yes," Ethan said bluntly, his voice cutting through her rising panic. "That's exactly what he's been doing. And that's why we have to stop him."

She stopped pacing, her hands balling into fists at her sides. "And how do we do that? He's not just some random doctor—he's the head of this hospital's emergency department. People respect him. Hell, I respected him. Who's going to believe he's behind something like this?"

"We make them believe it," Ethan said, his gaze steady. "With evidence. Proof they can't ignore."

Lily's laugh was sharp, almost bitter. "You mean the proof we're standing in right now? This hidden lab? These files? Do you really think that's going to be enough to bring him down?"

"It's a start," Ethan replied, his voice calm but unyielding. "And it's more than we had before."

She turned away, pressing a hand to her forehead as the weight of the revelation pressed down on her. "I don't know if I can do this. If I can face him knowing what I know now."

"You can," Ethan said firmly, stepping closer. "Because you have to. He's counting on you backing down, Lily. He's counting on you being too afraid, too conflicted to act. That's how people like him survive."

She turned back to him, her voice trembling with emotion. "But he's not just some faceless villain to me, Ethan. He's—he's Dr. Harlow. The man who talked me through my first trauma case. The man who made me believe I could actually do this job."

Ethan's gaze softened, and for a moment, the sharp edges of his demeanor dulled. "I get it. I do. But that man—the one you knew? He's gone. Whoever Harlow is now, he's not the person you admired. And the sooner you accept that, the sooner we can stop him."

Lily stared at him, her chest tight, her mind a storm of emotions she couldn't sort through. Finally, she nodded, her voice quiet but steady. "Okay. But this isn't just about stopping him. It's about making sure no one else gets hurt."

Ethan nodded, his voice carrying the weight of their shared resolve. "Agreed. And we start by taking this evidence and finding out exactly how deep this goes."

As they gathered the files, the sterile hum of the lab's equipment seemed louder now, a stark reminder of the lives that had already been affected by Harlow's actions. Lily's hands shook slightly as she picked up another stack of papers, but her resolve was growing stronger with every moment.

She glanced at Ethan, her voice quieter now. "We're going to need a plan."

"We'll make one," he replied, his tone steady. "And when we do, we'll make sure there's no way for him to escape this."

She nodded, her jaw tightening as a flicker of determination sparked in her chest. Dr. Harlow may have been her mentor, but now he was something else—an enemy hiding in plain sight. And she was going to do whatever it took to bring him down.

The hospital rooftop was quiet, the city below a canvas of flickering lights. Lily leaned against the railing, the cold metal grounding her as her thoughts churned. The file folder clutched in her hand felt heavier than it should have, the weight of its contents pressing down on her chest.

"You've been up here a while," Ethan's voice cut through the silence, calm but laced with concern.

She didn't turn to face him, her eyes fixed on the horizon. "Needed some air."

"Figured as much," he said, stepping closer but keeping a respectful distance. "Want to talk about it?"

Lily sighed, her voice tight. "What's there to talk about? Everything I thought I knew… it's all a lie."

Ethan leaned against the railing beside her, his gaze steady. "It's not all a lie."

She turned to him then, her eyes flashing with frustration. "Isn't it? Harlow was the one who taught me to trust my instincts, to fight for my patients. And now I find out he's been… experimenting on them? How do I reconcile that, Ethan?"

He didn't answer right away, his silence offering her space to continue.

"I used to watch him in the ER," she said, her voice quieter now. "He was always so calm, so precise. Even in the worst situations, he knew exactly what to do. I wanted to be like that. To have that kind of confidence."

"And now you feel like you've been duped," Ethan said softly.

She nodded, her throat tightening. "Every time I trusted him, every time I defended him—was I enabling this? Did I look the other way when I should've been asking questions?"

"You couldn't have known," Ethan said firmly. "He's been playing this game for a long time, Lily. People like him—they're good at hiding in plain sight."

"But I should've seen it," she said, her voice trembling with guilt. "There were moments, little things that didn't add up. Cases he dismissed too quickly, tests he ordered without explaining why. I brushed them off because I thought… because I believed he knew better."

"You believed in him," Ethan said, his tone softening. "There's no shame in that."

She laughed bitterly, shaking her head. "Isn't there? I built my entire career on this idea that medicine is noble, that it's about saving lives no matter what. And now? Now I see how easy it is for that to be corrupted. For people like Harlow to twist it into something monstrous."

Ethan turned to face her fully, his voice steady. "What Harlow's done doesn't erase what you've accomplished, Lily. You're still the doctor who fights for her patients, who goes above and beyond to save them. That hasn't changed."

She looked at him, her eyes shining with unshed tears. "But it feels different now. Like no matter how hard I try, it's not enough. Like I'm part of a system that lets this happen."

"You're not part of the problem," he said firmly. "You're part of the solution. You saw the cracks, and you're doing something about it. That's more than most people would do."

She exhaled slowly, her gaze dropping to the folder in her hands. "I keep wondering if there was ever a moment where he hesitated. Where he thought about stopping."

Ethan's jaw tightened, his voice taking on a harder edge. "Maybe. But even if he did, he still made the choice to keep going. And that's on him, not you."

Lily looked back at the city, her thoughts still tangled. "It's hard to accept that someone I admired so much could do something like this. It makes me question everything."

"That's how they get to you," Ethan said, his voice quieter now. "They make you doubt yourself, your instincts, your purpose. But you can't let that win."

She turned to him, her voice soft but laced with determination. "I don't know if I can ever forgive him—for what he's done, for what he's made me feel."

"You don't have to forgive him," Ethan said, his gaze steady. "You just have to stop him."

Lily nodded slowly, the weight in her chest easing just a fraction. "You make it sound so simple."

"It's not," Ethan admitted. "But that's why we're in this together."

She gave him a faint smile, her voice steadier now. "Thanks, Ethan. For… being here. For reminding me what matters."

He nodded, a flicker of warmth in his otherwise stoic expression. "Anytime, Doc."

As they stood there, side by side against the night sky, Lily felt a small spark of clarity. The betrayal still stung, and the guilt hadn't disappeared, but beneath it all was a growing resolve. She couldn't undo the past, but she could fight for the future. And that, she realized, was what mattered most.

Lily sat in the dimly lit corner of the hospital's staff lounge, her fingers tracing the edge of the file folder resting on the table. The air felt heavy, charged with the weight of decisions she couldn't avoid. Across from her, Ethan watched in silence, his calm presence an anchor against the storm raging in her chest.

"I thought this job was supposed to be about saving people," she said finally, her voice quiet but filled with a raw edge. "Not… this."

Ethan leaned forward, resting his forearms on the table. "It still is. What you're doing right now? That's saving people."

She looked up at him, her eyes clouded with doubt. "Is it? Or am I just chasing shadows? What if I make things worse?"

"You won't," Ethan said firmly. "You've already seen too much to turn back now. The only way to fix this is to keep going."

His certainty steadied her, and she nodded slowly, letting the resolve settle back into place. "Alright," she said, taking a deep breath. "So where do we start?"

Ethan reached for the file, flipping through its contents with practiced precision. "We've got evidence connecting Harlow to the lab and the tests. But it's not enough. We need to find out who he's working with, where the funding is coming from, and how far this goes."

Lily leaned over the table, her voice gaining strength. "The lab records—there were references to shipments. If we can trace where the materials are coming from, maybe we can find a link to whoever's backing this."

Ethan nodded, his lips pressing into a thin line. "That's good. The shipments might also lead us to where they're planning to deploy this thing. If we can intercept it…"

"We can stop it," Lily finished, her determination growing. She paused, her voice softening. "But what if we're too late? What if it's already out there?"

Ethan's jaw tightened, but his voice remained steady. "Then we'll deal with that when it happens. Right now, we focus on what we can control."

She let his words sink in, the pragmatic clarity of his approach helping to quiet the doubts clawing at her. She reached for her phone, scrolling through her notes. "I'll need to access the hospital's inventory system. If they've been using internal resources to supplement the lab, there might be records."

"Do it carefully," Ethan warned. "If Harlow or anyone else catches on to what you're doing, they'll shut us down before we can make a move."

Lily glanced up at him, her voice sharp. "You think I don't know that? Harlow already threatened me once. He's watching me—probably waiting for me to slip up."

Ethan's gaze softened. "Then don't give him the chance."

The quiet intensity of his words wrapped around her like a shield, and she nodded. "I won't."

They lapsed into silence, the hum of the lounge's refrigerator the only sound as they reviewed the evidence spread out between them. The enormity of their task loomed like a shadow, but Lily felt steadier with Ethan by her side, his focus and conviction grounding her.

After a while, she broke the silence, her voice quieter now. "This is going to change everything, isn't it?"

Ethan glanced at her, his expression unreadable. "It already has."

She swallowed hard, the weight of his words settling over her. "I don't know what I'll do when this is over. If it's over."

"You'll keep doing what you've always done," Ethan said, his voice unwavering. "You'll fight for your patients. For what's right. That's who you are, Lily."

His certainty warmed something inside her, a flicker of hope breaking through the doubt. "And what about you?" she asked, her tone lightening just a fraction. "What happens to you when this is over?"

Ethan hesitated, his gaze dropping to the table. "People like me don't get an 'after.' There's always another mission."

"That sounds lonely," she said softly, surprising herself with the vulnerability in her voice.

He looked up, his eyes meeting hers. "It is. But you get used to it."

Her chest tightened, but she didn't push further. Instead, she reached across the table, her hand brushing against his as she took one of the files. "Then let's make this one count."

Ethan's lips quirked into the faintest hint of a smile. "Deal."

As they packed up their evidence and prepared to move forward, Lily felt the weight of betrayal still pressing on her chest. But beneath it was something stronger—an unshakable resolve to see this through. Whatever dangers lay ahead, she wasn't facing them alone.

And that, she realized, made all the difference.

Chapter 8
The Cost of Secrets

The ER was a maelstrom of activity, the air charged with urgency and barely contained panic. Patients filled every bed, their groans and labored breaths weaving into the steady rhythm of monitors and distant voices. Nurses hurried between stations, their faces tight with focus, while doctors barked orders that barely pierced the chaos.

Lily stood at the foot of a patient's bed, flipping through the chart with shaky hands. The woman lying in front of her, a schoolteacher in her mid-thirties, was pale and drenched in sweat. Her oxygen levels were plummeting, despite the non-rebreather mask strapped to her face.

"Her fever's up to 104.8," Nina reported as she adjusted the IV.

Lily nodded, her throat dry. "Push another liter of saline and start her on broad-spectrum antibiotics. We'll get a culture and—"

"Already sent," Nina interrupted, her voice tight.

Lily moved to the next bed, where another patient, a teenage boy, coughed violently, his chest rattling with each wheezing breath. She caught Ethan's gaze from across the room. He was leaning casually against the wall, his eyes scanning the scene with an intensity that set her nerves on edge.

"Ethan," she called, motioning for him to follow her to a quieter corner near the supply room.

He approached slowly, his expression grim. "Busy morning," he remarked.

"This isn't normal," Lily snapped, her voice low. "None of this is normal."

Ethan tilted his head, a faint smirk tugging at the corner of his lips. "You're starting to see it."

"Stop being cryptic," she hissed, stepping closer. "These patients aren't just sick—they're crashing. And the treatments aren't working. Why aren't they working?"

Ethan glanced over his shoulder, ensuring no one was within earshot. "Because it's not about the treatments, Doc," he said softly. "It's about what they're fighting."

"And what exactly are they fighting?" Lily demanded.

He leaned in slightly, his voice barely above a whisper. "Something engineered. Something designed not to respond to what you're throwing at it."

Her breath hitched, and she took a step back. "That's… impossible. Pathogens don't just—"

"They do if someone makes them that way," Ethan interrupted, his tone cold.

Lily stared at him, her mind spinning. "You're saying this was deliberate? That someone—"

"Tested it," Ethan finished. "Right here, in your ER."

She shook her head, her disbelief colliding with the evidence she couldn't ignore. "That doesn't make sense. Why here? Why now?"

Ethan's gaze hardened. "Because hospitals are contained environments. Controlled chaos, remember? Perfect for studying outcomes."

"This isn't a lab!" she shot back, her frustration boiling over. "These are people's lives! Do you have any idea what's at stake?"

"Of course I do," Ethan replied, his voice rising just enough to make her flinch. He softened immediately, his tone shifting to something almost apologetic. "I get it, Lily. Believe me, I do. But this isn't just a hospital problem anymore. It's bigger than that."

Lily's hands clenched into fists at her sides. "And you knew this was happening? You knew, and you didn't stop it?"

"I didn't know it would be here," Ethan said quietly, his gaze dropping. "Not until it was too late."

"Then help me fix it," she said, her voice steady despite the panic threatening to bubble up. "If you know something—

anything—we can use to help these patients, you need to tell me. Now."

Ethan hesitated, his jaw tightening. "It's not that simple."

"It is that simple!" she snapped. "You either help me, or you stay out of my way. But don't stand here and act like you're some hero when you're holding back information that could save lives."

Ethan held her gaze for a long moment, his expression unreadable. Finally, he nodded. "Alright," he said. "I'll tell you what I can. But you have to promise me something first."

Lily folded her arms, her eyes narrowing. "What?"

"Once you know the truth," he said, his voice low, "you don't stop. No matter how dangerous it gets."

Her breath caught, the weight of his words sinking in. She nodded slowly, her voice barely above a whisper. "I promise."

Ethan straightened, his smirk returning but faint and humorless. "Good. Then let's get to work."

As they moved back into the chaos of the ER, Lily's mind churned with questions she didn't want to answer and fears she couldn't ignore. Whatever Ethan was hiding, it was clear they were running out of time.

Lily burst into Dr. Harlow's office, her clipboard clutched tightly in one hand. Her heart pounded in her chest, fueled by frustration and the mounting chaos in the ER. Dr. Harlow sat behind his desk, his glasses perched on the tip of his nose as he scrolled through a tablet.

"Dr. Harlow, we need to talk," Lily said, her voice sharp.

He barely glanced up. "I assumed as much, Dr. Chen. You usually knock."

Lily ignored the comment, stepping further into the room. "It's about the patients—the infections. We have multiple cases now with identical symptoms, and none of the treatments are working. This isn't a coincidence."

Dr. Harlow sighed, setting his tablet down with deliberate slowness. "It's flu season, Dr. Chen. People get sick. Treatments take time."

"This isn't the flu," Lily countered, her tone rising. "The symptoms are too severe, and they're escalating. We need to investigate—dig into the source before this gets any worse."

He leaned back in his chair, his expression calm but condescending. "And what would you suggest? A full epidemiological study in the middle of an ER shift? We don't have the resources or the time for that. Stick to what you're here to do—patient care."

Her jaw tightened, and she took a step closer to his desk. "You're not listening. If we don't act now, this could spiral out of control. People are already dying."

"And people will keep dying, Dr. Chen," he said bluntly. "That's the nature of this job. You can't save everyone."

The words hit her like a slap. "That's not the point, and you know it. If this outbreak is spreading, it's our responsibility to stop it."

Dr. Harlow finally looked up, his gaze steady but dismissive. "Your responsibility is to treat the patients in front of you. Let the higher-ups handle the rest."

Lily's breath caught, a mix of anger and disbelief swelling in her chest. "So we just ignore it? Wait until it's too late and hope someone else fixes the problem?"

"Dr. Chen," he said, his voice hardening, "I understand you're passionate about your work, but you need to focus on what's within your control. This isn't it."

She stared at him, her fists clenching at her sides. "With all due respect, Dr. Harlow, you're wrong."

His expression didn't waver. "Get back to your shift, Dr. Chen."

Lily turned on her heel, storming out of the office without another word. The door closed behind her with a sharp click, but the anger in her chest burned hotter with every step she took.

As she moved back toward the ER, her gaze caught on a figure leaning against the wall just outside the staff lounge. Ethan stood there, arms crossed, his dark eyes following her as she approached.

"Rough meeting?" he asked, his tone dry but not unkind.

"What do you think?" she snapped, her frustration spilling over.

Ethan pushed off the wall, falling into step beside her as she walked. "Let me guess. He told you to keep your head down and stay in your lane?"

"Pretty much," she said bitterly. "I tried to explain what's happening, but he doesn't want to listen. He's too busy writing it off as flu season to see what's right in front of him."

"Typical," Ethan said with a shrug.

Lily stopped abruptly, turning to face him. "This isn't funny, Ethan. People are dying, and he's doing nothing. How am I supposed to fix this when no one else cares?"

Ethan's expression softened, and for a moment, he looked almost sympathetic. "You care," he said simply.

"That's not enough," she shot back.

"Maybe not," he admitted. "But it's a start."

Lily shook her head, her frustration bubbling over again. "I need more than a start. I need answers. I need help. And I can't keep wasting time fighting with people who won't listen."

"Then stop fighting," Ethan said, his voice calm but firm.

"What's that supposed to mean?"

"It means you already know what's happening," he said, stepping closer. "You don't need their permission to figure out the rest. You just need to follow the trail."

"And what trail is that?" she asked, her voice tinged with suspicion.

Ethan's lips curved into a faint smirk. "You're already on it, Doc. Just keep going."

She stared at him, her chest tightening with the weight of his words. "Why do I feel like you're enjoying this?"

"Because I am," he admitted, his smirk widening slightly. "But that doesn't mean I'm wrong."

Lily exhaled sharply, turning away. "If I get fired for this, I'm blaming you."

"Fair enough," Ethan said lightly.

As she moved back into the chaos of the ER, Ethan lingered for a moment, his expression unreadable. Lily didn't need his cryptic remarks to tell her what she already knew—if she wanted to get to the bottom of this, she'd have to do it on her own.

The records room was dimly lit, the faint hum of the fluorescent bulbs above adding to the eerie quiet. Lily sat at a small desk, a pile of patient files spread out before her. Her eyes scanned each page quickly but meticulously, the details starting to blur together. Fever. Respiratory distress. Fatigue. The patterns were consistent, but something was missing.

She flipped to the next file, her pen tapping rhythmically against the desk. As she reached the lab orders, her pen stopped mid-tap. The requisition form was signed by Dr. Vega, but the test itself was unusual—an advanced genetic assay she'd only seen used in experimental research.

Frowning, she pulled another chart and another. The same test, the same signature, repeated across multiple cases. Her stomach twisted as realization dawned. This wasn't routine care. Someone had been digging deeper, using these patients for something else entirely.

Footsteps echoed faintly behind her, and she tensed, glancing over her shoulder. Ethan stood in the doorway, his figure half-shadowed.

"You always work this late?" he asked, his voice casual but his gaze sharp.

Lily gestured to the files. "What are you doing here?"

Ethan stepped into the room, leaning casually against the desk. "Just checking in. You looked… determined earlier."

She ignored his tone, shoving a file toward him. "Look at this."

He raised an eyebrow but took the file, flipping it open. His smirk faded as his eyes scanned the page. "Where'd you find this?"

"In the patient records," she said, her voice clipped. "Dr. Vega ordered advanced genetic assays for multiple patients—tests that aren't part of normal diagnostics. What does that tell you?"

Ethan's jaw tightened as he closed the file. "It tells me you're digging in the right place."

Her pulse quickened, and she leaned forward. "So it's true, isn't it? Someone's using these patients for more than treatment."

Ethan hesitated, his gaze dropping to the floor. "It looks that way."

"Don't do that," she snapped, frustration spilling over. "Stop pretending like you don't already know."

He met her eyes, the usual ease in his demeanor replaced with something harder. "Alright, you're right. I do know. But you need to be careful, Lily. This isn't just about the patients anymore."

She pushed her chair back, rising to her feet. "Then tell me what it's about. Who's behind this? Dr. Vega?"

"It's not just Vega," Ethan said, his tone lowering. "She's part of it, but this goes higher. A lot higher."

Lily's breath caught, and she shook her head. "That doesn't make sense. How could this go beyond the hospital? Why would anyone want to—"

"Test a pathogen?" Ethan finished for her. "Because it's the perfect environment. Controlled chaos, remember? Patients come in sick, they get worse, and no one questions it because it looks like nature."

Her chest tightened as the implications sank in. "And the genetic tests? What are they looking for?"

"Markers," Ethan said grimly. "They're trying to understand how it spreads, who it affects, and why."

Lily's hand clenched the edge of the desk. "You're saying this is deliberate. That someone's using these people as test subjects."

"That's exactly what I'm saying," Ethan replied.

She stared at him, her mind racing. "And you knew this was happening?"

"Not here," he said quickly. "Not until now. But I've seen it before, in other places."

"Why didn't you stop it?" she demanded.

"I tried," Ethan said, his voice tight. "But these people—they're powerful. They cover their tracks, and anyone who gets too close…"

His words trailed off, the weight of his silence filling the room.

"You think I'm in danger," Lily said quietly.

"I know you are," he said, stepping closer. "You're in over your head, Doc. These people don't play fair, and they don't leave loose ends."

She met his gaze, her fear mingling with defiance. "If you think I'm going to stop, you're wrong."

"Lily," he said, his voice softening. "I'm not telling you to stop. I'm telling you to be smart. If you're going to keep digging, you need to watch your back."

She crossed her arms, her resolve hardening. "Then help me."

He hesitated, studying her for a long moment. Finally, he nodded. "Alright. But if we're doing this, we do it my way. No unnecessary risks."

Lily exhaled, a mix of relief and apprehension washing over her. "Deal."

As Ethan turned to leave, he paused in the doorway. "One more thing," he said, his tone lighter but no less serious. "If anyone asks, you found this on your own. Keep my name out of it."

She smirked faintly. "You're good at staying in the shadows, aren't you?"

"Better than you think," he replied with a wink before disappearing into the hallway.

Lily sank back into her chair, her mind churning with questions. The discovery felt like the first piece of a much larger puzzle, and she wasn't sure she was ready for what the rest of it would reveal.

The steady beeping of monitors in the ER was a familiar backdrop for Lily as she checked her patient's vitals. The elderly woman had seemed stable just hours earlier—her fever had subsided, and her breathing, while labored, had shown signs of improvement. But now, her chest rose and fell unevenly, her oxygen levels dropping on the monitor's screen.

"Nina," Lily called, her voice tense.

Nina appeared at her side instantly, her expression mirroring Lily's concern. "She was fine an hour ago," Nina said, adjusting the oxygen flow.

"She's not fine now," Lily replied, her hands moving swiftly to assess the woman's condition.

The woman's eyes fluttered open briefly, her lips moving soundlessly. Lily leaned closer. "Mrs. Keller, can you hear me?"

A faint, rattling sound escaped the patient's lips—a desperate attempt at speech that ended in a violent cough.

"We're losing her," Lily muttered, her voice sharp with urgency. "Let's intubate—get the crash cart."

Before Nina could respond, the monitor emitted a flat, piercing tone.

"No," Lily whispered, the weight of the sound hitting her like a blow. "No, no, no!"

The room exploded into motion. Nina brought the crash cart while Lily initiated CPR, pressing against the frail chest beneath her hands.

"Come on," Lily pleaded, her voice cracking. "Come on, don't do this."

The team worked in practiced unison, but after what felt like an eternity, Nina placed a hand on Lily's shoulder.

"She's gone," Nina said softly.

Lily froze, her hands still on the woman's chest. The room fell silent except for the mournful beep of the flatline. Slowly, Lily stepped back, her breath hitching as she stared at the lifeless figure on the bed.

She found Ethan in the corridor just outside the ER, his expression unreadable as he leaned against the wall. The faint buzz of fluorescent lights above only deepened the shadows around him.

“I lost her,” Lily said, her voice hollow.

Ethan straightened, his eyes locking onto hers. “I know.”

“How?” she asked, the frustration and grief twisting in her voice. “How did this happen? She was stable. She should’ve been getting better.”

“She didn’t stand a chance,” Ethan said quietly.

Lily’s jaw tightened, her fists clenching at her sides. “What are you talking about?”

Ethan hesitated, glancing around to ensure they were alone. “This isn’t just a virus, Lily. It’s not a natural outbreak.”

She stepped closer, her voice rising. “Then what is it? What’s killing these people?”

Ethan met her gaze, his expression grim. “It’s a weapon.”

The words felt like a slap, and for a moment, she couldn’t breathe. “A weapon? You’re saying this was deliberate?”

“That’s exactly what I’m saying,” Ethan replied.

Her mind raced, the weight of his words crashing over her. “Who would do something like this? And why here?”

"Because it's the perfect testing ground," Ethan said, his tone laced with bitterness. "People come in sick, they get worse, and no one questions it. It's chaos disguised as routine."

Lily shook her head, the disbelief warring with the evidence she couldn't ignore. "This can't be real. This can't be happening."

"It is," Ethan said firmly. "And if we don't stop it, more people are going to die."

She stared at him, her chest tightening with a mix of fear and determination. "You knew," she said softly. "You knew this was happening, and you didn't tell me."

"I didn't have proof," he said, his voice heavy. "Not until now."

"And now?"

"Now, we fight back," Ethan said. "But I can't do it alone."

Lily exhaled sharply, her emotions threatening to overwhelm her. "I don't even know where to start."

"You start by trusting me," Ethan said.

Her eyes narrowed. "That's a big ask, coming from someone who's spent more time dodging my questions than answering them."

"I didn't tell you everything because I didn't want to put you in danger," Ethan said, his voice softening. "But you're already in it, Lily. Whether you like it or not."

She looked away, her mind churning. She thought of Mrs. Keller, of the other patients who were still fighting for their lives. Ethan was right—this wasn't just a hospital problem anymore.

Finally, she met his gaze. "Alright," she said, her voice steady despite the storm inside her. "I'm in. But if we do this, we do it my way. No more secrets."

Ethan nodded, a faint smile flickering across his face. "Deal."

As they stood there in the dim corridor, the weight of their decision settled over them. The stakes had never been higher, and the path ahead was shrouded in uncertainty. But for the first time, they stood on the same side, ready to face whatever came next.

Chapter 9
Unraveling the Threads

The quiet hum of the hospital's administrative wing was a stark contrast to the turmoil roiling within Lily. She sat at a corner desk in the deserted records office, the soft glow of her laptop illuminating the furrow in her brow. Stacks of patient files surrounded her like sentinels, each one a silent testament to the lives that had been quietly manipulated.

Ethan leaned against the wall behind her, his arms crossed and his gaze fixed on the door. His presence was steady, reassuring, but the tension in his shoulders betrayed his vigilance.

"This is the fifth case that matches," Lily murmured, her voice hushed but sharp. She flipped through another chart, her fingers moving with the precision of a surgeon. "Same symptoms—fever, respiratory failure, unexplained immune suppression. The treatment protocols don't add up."

Ethan stepped closer, the shadow he cast over the desk making her glance up briefly. "And the common denominator?" he asked, his tone measured but expectant.

"Lab work," she said, pointing to a section of the file. "Every one of these patients had blood cultures and pathogen screenings done by the same technician: Markus Shaw."

Ethan's eyes narrowed, his mind already piecing together the implications. "Shaw. Is he senior enough to be in on this, or just a pawn?"

Lily hesitated, scanning another document. "He's experienced—mid-level, but with enough clearance to handle dangerous pathogens. Look at this." She turned the screen toward him, highlighting a line in the records. "He processed samples for Margaret Fields and Casey Thompson. The same week he handled two other patients who showed similar symptoms."

"And those samples went to the restricted lab," Ethan said, his voice sharpening. "He's involved, whether he knows the full extent or not."

Lily leaned back, the weight of their discovery settling over her. "If he's the link, then confronting him could blow this wide open. But it could also push whoever's behind this into overdrive."

Ethan moved to her side, his presence grounding her as she turned her attention back to the files. "We don't confront him," he said. "Not yet. We track his movements, see who he's working with. If Shaw's our connection to Harlow's operation, we can't risk tipping him off."

She nodded, her fingers brushing across the edge of the desk as she processed his words. "There's another thing," she said, her tone quieter now. "Shaw's name shows up on records for patients who weren't part of the usual hospital intake."

Ethan tilted his head, his gaze sharpening. "What do you mean?"

"These patients were transferred here from smaller clinics or out-of-town facilities," Lily explained, pulling up a new document. "It's like someone cherry-picked them for testing."

Ethan's jaw tightened, his mind racing. "That means Harlow isn't just working with Shaw—he's coordinating with outside sources. This goes beyond the hospital."

The implications settled heavily between them, the air in the room seeming to thicken. Lily ran a hand through her hair, her frustration bubbling over. "How far does this go, Ethan? Every time we think we're getting closer, it just… expands."

Ethan crouched beside her, his voice steady but firm. "It goes as far as we let it. And right now, we've got leverage. These records—they're not just evidence. They're a map."

She met his gaze, the intensity in his eyes sparking something within her. "And Shaw's our guide."

"Exactly," Ethan said, standing and pacing to the window. He stared out at the dimly lit parking lot below, his tone turning contemplative. "But we have to move carefully. If we make the wrong move, we lose him—and any chance we have of stopping this."

Lily's gaze drifted back to the files, her mind spinning with possibilities. "What if we trace his workflow? See who he reports to, who he interacts with most."

"That's a start," Ethan agreed, turning back to her. "But we also need eyes on him. If Shaw's meeting with anyone outside the hospital, it could lead us straight to Harlow's backers."

Her stomach twisted at the thought of going deeper into the shadows they were uncovering, but she nodded, her resolve hardening. "Then we track him. But we can't wait too long. If he's part of the team refining this pathogen, they're already ahead of us."

Ethan crossed his arms, his expression unreadable as he studied her. "You're holding up well, Doc. Better than most people would in your position."

She glanced at him, her lips curving into a faint smile despite the weight pressing on her chest. "I don't think I have much of a choice, do I?"

"No," he said simply, his voice carrying a quiet respect. "But you're doing more than holding on. You're fighting."

She didn't reply, her attention returning to the files as she absorbed his words. The stakes were higher than ever, but so was her determination. Shaw was their next lead—a key piece in a puzzle that was quickly becoming clearer.

"We're getting close," Ethan said, his voice steady but laced with urgency. "Close enough that they'll start making moves to protect themselves."

Lily nodded, her voice firm. "Then we need to move faster."

The two of them exchanged a brief glance, a silent understanding passing between them. There was no turning back now. Every step they took brought them closer to the truth—and deeper into the danger waiting just ahead.

The hospital's rooftop was bathed in soft moonlight, the faint hum of the city below muffled by the height. Lily stood near the railing, the cool night air brushing against her skin. She gripped the edge tightly, her knuckles white as she stared at the horizon. The tension in her chest refused to ease, no matter how deeply she tried to breathe.

Behind her, Ethan's footsteps were soft, measured. He stopped a few feet away, his voice breaking the silence. "You've been quiet since we found Shaw's connection."

She didn't turn around. "Quiet doesn't mean I'm not thinking."

"I know," he said, his tone gentler now. "But thinking like this, alone in the dark, usually means the thoughts aren't good."

Lily let out a bitter laugh, her grip tightening. "When are they ever? We're uncovering something monstrous, Ethan. Every file, every patient—it's like peeling back layers of a nightmare I didn't know I was living in."

He stepped closer, his hands in his pockets. "You're not living in it alone."

She turned then, her face illuminated by the faint glow of the city lights. Her eyes glistened, and her voice trembled. "That's the thing—I've never felt more alone. Everything I thought I knew, everything I believed in, it's all falling apart. Medicine, this hospital, Harlow—it's all poisoned."

Ethan's expression softened, his voice steady. "It's not all poisoned. You're still here. You still care."

Her laugh was sharp, self-deprecating. "Caring doesn't fix this. Caring doesn't undo what's already been done."

"No," Ethan agreed, moving closer. "But it keeps you in the fight. And right now, that's what matters."

Lily shook her head, her voice breaking. "I'm so scared, Ethan. Not just of what we'll find, but of what it's doing to me. To us. Every day, it feels like I'm losing pieces of myself."

"You're not," he said firmly, stepping into her space. "You're holding onto what matters. That's why you're still standing."

She met his eyes, her chest tightening. "But what if I can't? What if this breaks me?"

Ethan reached out, his hand brushing lightly against her arm. "It won't. You're stronger than you think."

She laughed softly, the sound tinged with disbelief. "You always say that."

"Because it's true," he said, his voice quieter now, almost a whisper. "You don't see it, but I do. Every time you fight for those patients, every time you push back against the fear—you prove it."

Her breath caught, the sincerity in his words cutting through her defenses. "And you? How do you keep going?"

Ethan hesitated, his gaze dropping for a moment before returning to hers. "I focus on the mission. On what's right in front of me. And right now, that's you."

The air between them shifted, the tension taking on a new weight. Lily's heart raced as his words settled over her, their meaning clear in the way he looked at her—as though she were the only thing grounding him in the chaos.

"Ethan…" she began, her voice faltering.

He stepped closer, his hand cupping her cheek with a gentleness that caught her off guard. "Lily, you don't have to carry this alone. We're in this together."

Her breath hitched, and for a moment, the world fell away. The weight of their shared mission, the danger that loomed over them—it all faded, leaving only the electric connection between them. Slowly, hesitantly, Ethan leaned in.

Their lips met in a brief, intense kiss, a collision of fear, longing, and unspoken promises. The contact was soft but charged, a silent acknowledgment of everything they'd been holding back.

When they pulled apart, Lily's eyes searched his, her voice barely above a whisper. "That wasn't… what I expected."

Ethan smirked faintly, his hand still lingering on her cheek. "Me neither."

She let out a soft laugh, the tension in her chest easing slightly. "But I'm glad it happened."

"So am I," he said, his tone low but steady.

For a moment, they stood there in silence, the weight of the world creeping back in but somehow feeling lighter. Lily exhaled, stepping back slightly but keeping her gaze locked with his.

"We should… get back to work," she said, though her voice lacked conviction.

Ethan nodded, his expression softening. "Yeah. But we'll get through this, Lily. Together."

She smiled faintly, the warmth of his words settling in her chest. "Together."

As they left the rooftop, their resolve felt stronger, bolstered by the connection that had finally broken through the fear. The road ahead was still uncertain, but for the first time, Lily felt like she wasn't walking it alone.

The hospital corridors felt colder in the quiet hours of the night. Lily walked beside Ethan, her steps quick and purposeful. Neither of them spoke as they headed toward the records office, the silence between them charged with the unspoken weight of what had just passed between them.

Ethan broke the silence first, his voice calm but clipped. "We need to find out how Shaw is moving these samples. If he's working alone or if someone else is covering for him."

Lily nodded, her fingers curling into fists at her sides. "The logs in the lab will show his access history. If we can cross-reference that with the patient files…"

Her words trailed off as they rounded the corner, and Ethan glanced at her, his brow furrowing. "Lily."

"What?" she asked, her voice sharper than she intended. She glanced at him, her pulse skipping as their eyes met. His gaze was steady, searching, and it made her chest tighten.

"Are you okay?" he asked quietly.

She exhaled sharply, brushing a strand of hair behind her ear. "I'm fine. I just—look, what happened up there…" Her voice wavered, and she cleared her throat. "We don't have time to unpack it."

Ethan's lips quirked into the faintest of smirks. "Fair enough. But if you're fine, stop twisting your hands like you're bracing for impact."

Lily glanced down at her hands, realizing she'd been fidgeting, and quickly dropped them to her sides. "Noted," she muttered, her tone softening. "Let's just focus."

"Already there," he replied, his expression shifting back to business. "Shaw's our link, but if he gets wind that we're onto him, this whole thing falls apart."

Lily quickened her pace, her thoughts racing. "Then we make sure he doesn't. Start with the access logs, look for anomalies, and track where the samples went after they left his hands."

"Good," Ethan said, keeping pace with her. "And if the logs don't tell us enough?"

"Then we go straight to the source," she said, her voice hardening. "We find Shaw and figure out how deep he's in."

Ethan arched a brow. "That's bold, Doc. You sure you're ready for that?"

She stopped short, turning to face him. "No. But it doesn't matter, does it? We're running out of options, and if Shaw's the key to stopping this, I'll do whatever it takes."

For a moment, Ethan just looked at her, his expression unreadable. Then he nodded, his voice softening. "I know you will."

The quiet sincerity in his tone made her chest tighten again, and she looked away quickly, focusing on the hallway ahead. "Let's get those logs."

They entered the records office, the sterile light overhead flickering as Ethan locked the door behind them. Lily moved to the computer terminal, her fingers flying over the keyboard as she navigated the system. Ethan stood nearby, his eyes scanning the room as though expecting an ambush.

"Here," Lily said, pointing to the screen. "Shaw logged into the restricted lab at least six times this week. Each time corresponds to a patient we flagged."

Ethan leaned over her shoulder, his eyes narrowing as he studied the screen. "And the timestamps? Do they line up with when the samples were processed?"

Lily clicked through a few more files, her brow furrowing. "They do. But look at this—there's a gap. Two patients didn't go through the usual channels. Their samples bypassed the hospital's tracking system entirely."

"Which means someone's helping him," Ethan said grimly. "Shaw's not just a pawn—he's part of the mechanism."

Lily's stomach twisted as she scrolled through more data. "The samples were signed out under a different name. Not Shaw's."

"Whose?" Ethan asked, his voice low and steady.

She hesitated, her eyes narrowing at the screen. "It's… Dr. Harlow."

Ethan straightened, his jaw tightening. "Of course it is."

Lily leaned back, the air in the room feeling heavier. "It's like he's daring us to find him. Leaving just enough of a trail to keep us chasing but not enough to pin him down."

"Then we change the game," Ethan said, his tone sharp. "No more chasing. We set the terms."

Lily glanced up at him, her expression hardening. "How?"

He stepped back, crossing his arms as he considered their options. "We start with Shaw. If he's involved at this level, he knows more than he's letting on. And if he knows, we'll get it out of him."

She exhaled slowly, her fingers brushing against the edge of the desk. "We're walking a tightrope, Ethan. One wrong move…"

"We're not falling," he said firmly. "Not if we stick together."

Lily nodded, the tension in her chest easing slightly. "Alright. Let's do this."

As they gathered their findings, the unspoken connection between them lingered, fueling their resolve. The kiss had shifted something—deepened the trust, heightened the stakes. Neither of them spoke of it, but its impact was undeniable. They weren't just partners now; they were bound by something stronger, something that gave them the strength to face whatever lay ahead.

The small office was dim, lit only by the pale blue glow of the computer screen and the muted overhead light. Papers were spread haphazardly across the desk as Lily and Ethan worked side by side, their focus unwavering despite the hour. The silence between them was thick, broken only by the occasional rustle of paper or the tapping of keys.

Lily frowned, her eyes scanning the screen with growing unease. "Ethan, look at this."

He shifted closer, his sharp gaze narrowing as he followed her finger. "Another cluster?"

She nodded, her voice tight. "Three new cases in the last 48 hours. Same symptoms—fever, respiratory failure, immune suppression. But look at the timelines. The onset is faster, the progression more severe."

Ethan leaned over her, his jaw tightening. "They're accelerating."

Lily exhaled shakily, her stomach twisting. "If this isn't stopped, we're looking at a full-scale outbreak. These patients were already hospitalized when symptoms hit. Imagine what happens if this spreads outside these walls."

He stepped back, running a hand through his hair. "It's not just possible—it's the plan. Refine the pathogen here, test its limits, then take it into the wild."

Her chest tightened as the weight of his words settled over her. "How do you know?"

Ethan's voice was steady, but there was a cold edge to it. "Because that's how they work. You perfect the weapon in a controlled environment, then release it where it can't be traced back to you."

Lily turned away from the screen, her hands gripping the edge of the desk. "We've been thinking of this as a hospital problem. But it's so much bigger than that. If this gets out…"

"It's catastrophic," Ethan finished grimly. He moved to the window, staring out into the dark parking lot below. "And that's exactly what they want."

She followed him, her arms crossed tightly over her chest. "But why? What could they possibly gain from unleashing something like this?"

Ethan glanced at her, his expression hardening. "Control. Fear. Money. It doesn't matter. What matters is stopping it."

Lily shook her head, her voice trembling. "We're running out of time. The infections are coming faster, hitting harder. If we don't act now—"

"We will," he interrupted, his tone firm but not unkind. "But we have to be smart about this. If we rush in without a plan, we'll lose whatever edge we have."

She looked at him, her frustration bubbling over. "And what edge is that, Ethan? Harlow's got resources, connections, an entire network backing him. What do we have? A handful of files and a gut feeling?"

"We have the truth," he said simply, his gaze steady. "And that's more dangerous than anything they have."

Lily let out a bitter laugh, turning back to the desk. "You make it sound so easy. Like exposing them will magically fix everything."

"It won't," Ethan admitted, moving to stand beside her. "But it'll stop this. It'll save lives."

Her shoulders sagged, and she rested her hands on the desk, her voice quieter now. "Every time I think we're making progress, the scope of this just… expands. It feels like we're fighting a losing battle."

"You're not losing," he said, his voice softer now. "You're holding the line. And that's what matters."

She glanced at him, the sincerity in his tone catching her off guard. "You really believe that?"

"I do," he said firmly. "Because I've seen what happens when no one fights back. And I'm not letting that happen again."

Lily's chest tightened, the fear and determination warring within her. She looked down at the files spread across the desk, the weight of what they'd uncovered pressing heavily on her. "These patients—Margaret, Casey, the others—they deserved better than this."

"And because of you, they'll get it," Ethan said, his tone unwavering. "But only if we keep moving."

She nodded slowly, her resolve hardening. "You're right. We can't stop now."

Ethan placed a hand on her shoulder, his touch grounding her. "We won't. But we have to be ready for what's coming next."

She met his gaze, her voice steady despite the fear simmering beneath the surface. "Whatever it is, we'll face it. Together."

A faint smile tugged at his lips, though his eyes remained serious. "Damn right we will."

As they turned back to the files, a newfound urgency settled over them. The clock was ticking, and the stakes had never been higher. They didn't know what lay ahead, but one thing was certain: they were in this fight to the end, no matter the cost.

Chapter 10
Unmasking the Operative

The staff lounge door was slightly ajar, just enough for Lily to hear the murmur of Ethan's voice inside. She paused, her hand hovering over the handle as she strained to make out the words.

"…too close to move yet," Ethan said, his tone low and urgent.

There was a pause, followed by another hushed phrase she couldn't quite catch.

"…tracking the operative…"

Lily's pulse quickened. She pressed herself closer to the door, her mind racing. Operative? What operative?

The conversation ended abruptly, the sound of footsteps approaching the door snapping her out of her thoughts. She barely had time to step back before Ethan emerged, his face set in a grim mask.

"Who were you talking to?" she demanded, folding her arms across her chest.

Ethan stopped in his tracks, his dark eyes narrowing slightly. "Lily."

"Don't 'Lily' me," she shot back, her voice firm. "Who was it? What's going on?"

He sighed, glancing around the hallway before stepping closer. "It's time you knew," he said quietly, his usual guarded demeanor slipping just enough for her to see the tension beneath it. "There's someone inside this hospital—an operative. They're spreading the pathogen deliberately."

Her stomach dropped, a cold dread settling over her. "Deliberately?" she repeated, her voice barely above a whisper.

Ethan nodded, his expression grim. "This isn't an accident. The outbreak, the infections—it's all being orchestrated."

"Do you know who it is?" she asked, her voice rising with urgency.

He hesitated, the pause speaking louder than words. "I have my suspicions," he admitted. "But until I'm certain, I can't act."

"That's not good enough," Lily said sharply. "People are dying, Ethan. If you know something, you need to tell me—now."

"Do you think I don't know what's at stake?" he snapped back, his voice low but fierce. "Every move I make has to be precise. If I'm wrong—"

"Then figure it out," she interrupted, her frustration bubbling over. "Because I can't just stand by while this hospital turns into ground zero for something we don't understand."

Ethan studied her for a moment, his jaw tightening. "You're right," he said finally. "But you need to be careful, Lily. If you push too hard, you'll end up a target too."

Her breath caught, the weight of his words settling over her like a lead blanket. "I'm already involved," she said quietly. "So tell me what I need to know."

For a moment, it looked like he might. His lips parted, but then he closed them again, his eyes darting down the hallway. "Not here," he said. "Not now."

Before she could protest, he turned and walked away, leaving her standing in the hallway with more questions than answers.

Later that day, Lily stood at the nurses' station, her gaze drifting toward Dr. Vega, who was reviewing a patient chart across the room. The attending physician's expression was carefully composed, but something about her movements felt off—too calculated, too precise.

"Dr. Vega," a nurse called, handing her a file.

"Order another round of tests," Vega said, her tone crisp.

"Another round?" the nurse asked, frowning. "We've already run—"

"I said order the tests," Vega interrupted, her voice sharper than usual.

Lily's stomach twisted. The tests Vega was ordering weren't necessary—she knew that much. But the tension in Vega's shoulders, the way her fingers tapped against the edge of the chart, betrayed something more.

Was she nervous? Or was it something worse?

Ethan's warning echoed in her mind, seeding doubts that refused to be silenced. Deliberately. Operative. Target. Her trust in Dr. Vega, once unshakable, now wavered under the weight of suspicion. As she watched Vega disappear down the hall, Lily's professional instincts clashed with the growing dread inside her. If Ethan was right—and everything she'd seen today suggested he was—then the threat wasn't just real. It was standing right in front of her.

Lily couldn't ignore it anymore. She slipped quietly into the records room and began pulling patient charts, searching for patterns she hadn't noticed before. The unease she felt watching Vega earlier had taken root, and with each chart she flipped through, it grew. As the minutes ticked by, the evidence started to take shape—unnecessary tests, unusual lab requisitions, all tied back to Dr. Vega.

The door creaked open, and Lily jumped, clutching the chart in her hands. Ethan stood in the doorway, his expression unreadable.

"You found something," he said, stepping inside.

Lily nodded, handing him the chart. "Look at this. The tests, the requisitions—they all lead back to her."

Ethan flipped through the pages, his jaw tightening. "This is it," he said quietly. "This is what we needed."

"What do we do now?" Lily asked, her voice trembling.

Ethan looked up, his eyes meeting hers. "Now? We end this."

The soft hum of fluorescent lights buzzed faintly in the background as Lily flipped through the patient records on the computer screen. Her brow furrowed in concentration, her fingers flying over the keyboard as she navigated between test results and requisition forms. Ethan stood beside her, his arms crossed, his sharp gaze following every move she made.

"Here," Lily said, her voice tight as she tapped the monitor. "Every patient with these symptoms—fever, respiratory distress, rapid decline. Look at the labs. They all trace back to the same department."

Ethan leaned over her shoulder, his face darkening as he studied the data. "And all signed off by Dr. Vega," he said grimly, his tone heavy with implication.

"That doesn't prove anything," Lily countered, though her voice faltered as she spoke. "She's the attending for half the patients in this hospital. It could be coincidence."

Ethan straightened, his arms unfolding as he paced the small room. "It could be," he admitted, his voice softening. "But you know it's not."

Lily's hands stilled on the keyboard, her mind racing. She wanted to argue, to dismiss his words as paranoia, but the evidence was beginning to form a pattern she couldn't ignore.

The same tests ordered repeatedly without clear justification. Results that didn't align with standard protocols.

"Look at this," she said suddenly, pointing to a line of data. "Lab orders submitted under Vega's name, but no follow-up tests. No consultations. Just… nothing."

Ethan moved closer, scanning the screen. "Missing samples," he said, his jaw tightening. "They were submitted, but there's no record of what happened to them after that."

Lily's stomach churned as she clicked through more files, the discrepancies stacking up like a house of cards. "Delays in reporting. Incomplete notes." She shook her head, the weight of it settling over her. "This doesn't make sense. Why would she—"

Ethan cut her off, his tone sharper now. "Because she's covering something up. Or someone is."

"That's a big leap," Lily said, her voice trembling slightly. "We don't know that for sure."

"Lily," Ethan said, his voice softening again, "you're not the kind of person to ignore your gut. And your gut's telling you the same thing mine is."

She sighed, leaning back in her chair. "What if we're wrong? What if we're chasing shadows and we ruin someone's career in the process?"

Ethan crouched beside her, meeting her eyes. "And what if we're right? What if we do nothing, and more people die because of it?"

The question hung in the air, the weight of it pressing down on her. Lily looked back at the screen, her eyes scanning the list of patients, each name a stark reminder of what was at stake.

"We need more," she said finally, her voice steady but low. "If we're going to accuse her—or anyone—we need more than just patterns and suspicions."

Ethan nodded, standing again. "Then we keep digging. There's more here, I can feel it."

They worked in tense silence, the quiet punctuated only by the soft clicks of the keyboard and the occasional rustle of papers. As they dug deeper, the cracks in the facade became more apparent. Test samples that should have been logged were missing entirely. Lab results showed inexplicable anomalies that no one had flagged.

"Here," Ethan said, pointing to another entry on the screen. "This patient—tests were ordered, but there's no follow-up at all. The file just… ends."

Lily stared at the screen, her chest tightening. "That patient died," she said quietly. "And no one asked why."

Ethan's expression hardened. "Because someone didn't want them to."

She closed her eyes briefly, the implications hitting too close to home. "If this is true—if Vega's involved…"

Ethan placed a hand on the back of her chair, his tone firm but not unkind. "Then we do what we have to do. For them. For every patient who trusted this place to save them."

Lily opened her eyes, her resolve hardening. "We need to bring this to someone higher up. But if they're part of it—"

"Then we find another way," Ethan said, cutting her off. "But first, we gather everything we can. No gaps, no holes they can slip through."

She nodded, her hands returning to the keyboard. The weight of what they were uncovering pressed heavily on her, but she couldn't stop now. Not when the lives of so many people were hanging in the balance. As they worked side by side, a silent understanding passed between them.

Whatever this was, they were in it together. And there was no turning back.

The fluorescent-lit hallway buzzed with the usual activity of the morning shift—nurses hurrying to their stations, patients being wheeled to diagnostics, and the hum of conversation. Lily spotted Dr. Vega near the elevator bank, her composed figure standing out against the flurry of motion. Taking a deep breath, Lily clutched the file in her hand and strode forward.

"Dr. Vega," she called, trying to keep her voice even.

Vega turned slowly, her sharp features unreadable. "Dr. Chen," she said, her tone polite but clipped. "What can I do for you?"

Lily swallowed hard, forcing her nerves to stay in check. "Do you have a moment to talk?"

"Of course," Vega replied, though the slight lift of her brow hinted at impatience. "What's on your mind?"

Lily held up the file. "These lab orders," she began, her voice steady despite the thundering of her heart. "You signed them, but there's no record of follow-ups. And the patients—"

Vega's lips pressed into a thin smile, the kind that didn't reach her eyes. "Clerical errors, I'm sure," she said smoothly. "You know how it is in a busy hospital. Paperwork gets messy."

"But these aren't just errors," Lily pressed, her voice firming. "They're patterns."

For the briefest moment, something flickered across Vega's face—fear? Guilt? Lily couldn't be sure. But just as quickly as it appeared, it was replaced by a hard, impenetrable edge.

"You're new here, Dr. Chen," Vega said icily, her voice low enough that only Lily could hear. "I suggest you focus on your patients and leave the investigations to those qualified to conduct them."

Lily bristled, stepping closer. "With all due respect, this isn't about me being new. Patients are dying, Dr. Vega. And these discrepancies—"

"Are nothing more than coincidences," Vega interrupted, her tone growing sharper. "I've been at this hospital for years. I know the protocols, the systems. And I certainly don't need a first-year attending telling me how to do my job."

Lily's grip tightened on the file, her frustration bubbling over. "This isn't about protocol—it's about doing what's right. If there's even a chance that something's wrong, we owe it to these patients to find out."

Vega's eyes narrowed, her voice dropping to a dangerous whisper. "Be careful, Dr. Chen. Accusations like that can ruin careers. Yours included."

The threat hung in the air, chilling in its subtlety.

"This isn't a personal attack," Lily said, her voice trembling but resolute. "This is about the truth. If you have nothing to hide, then there shouldn't be a problem looking into this further."

Vega's lips curled into a cold smile. "You're ambitious, I'll give you that. But ambition without discretion is reckless. Remember that."

Without another word, Vega turned and walked away, her heels clicking against the tile floor. Lily stood frozen, the file still clutched tightly in her hand. The confidence she had mustered to confront Vega now felt shaken, battered by the weight of the conversation.

But the fear in Vega's eyes—brief as it had been—lingered in Lily's mind. It wasn't the response of someone with nothing to hide.

As Vega disappeared down the hallway, Ethan stepped out of the shadows, his expression grim. "How'd it go?"

Lily exhaled sharply, her grip on the file loosening. "She deflected, denied everything. But there's something there, Ethan. I know it."

"Of course there is," he said quietly. "But she's not going to make it easy for you. People like her never do."

"She threatened me," Lily said, her voice barely above a whisper.

Ethan's jaw tightened. "That's how you know you're getting close."

Lily looked up at him, her resolve hardening. "Then we keep pushing."

Ethan nodded, his dark eyes gleaming with determination. "We keep pushing."

As they moved back toward the records room, Lily's confidence began to steady. Vega's words had been a warning, yes, but they were also a confirmation. Something was deeply wrong, and now Lily was more determined than ever to uncover the truth—even if it meant risking everything.

The parking lot was dimly lit, the harsh yellow glow of the overhead lamps barely cutting through the evening shadows. Lily stood near a row of parked cars, her arms crossed tightly against her chest. Her heart pounded in her ears, drowning out the distant hum of traffic.

Ethan stepped out from the shadows, his figure blending effortlessly with the darkness. His movements were deliberate, but there was a tension in his shoulders she hadn't seen before.

"She knows I'm onto her," Lily said as soon as he was close enough to hear.

Ethan nodded, his face grim. "I suspected Vega, but this confirms it. She's been manipulating labs to hide the pathogen's origin."

Lily's breath caught, her mind racing. "The lab orders, the missing samples—it's all part of her cover-up, isn't it?"

"Exactly," Ethan said, his tone clipped. "She's been burying the data, keeping anyone from seeing the full picture."

"And the pathogen?" Lily asked, her voice trembling.

Ethan hesitated, his jaw tightening. "It's worse than we thought," he admitted finally. "This isn't just some rogue experiment or medical malpractice. It's a bioweapon, designed for targeted attacks. And Vega's just a cog in a much bigger machine."

Lily's knees felt weak, and she leaned against the nearest car for support. The weight of his words pressed down on her like a lead blanket, suffocating in its intensity. "A bioweapon," she repeated, her voice barely above a whisper.

Ethan stepped closer, his expression softening slightly. "I didn't want to tell you until I was sure, but you had to know. We're not dealing with random accidents or negligence. This is deliberate."

The revelation twisted in Lily's chest, her emotions warring between fear and anger. "And Vega's part of it?"

"She's complicit," Ethan said. "But she's not the mastermind. She's following orders, covering tracks, and keeping the operation running smoothly. But there's someone above her pulling the strings."

Lily shook her head, her hands gripping the edge of the car. "How could she do this? She's a doctor—she took an oath to save lives, not destroy them."

"People like Vega don't think like you do," Ethan said. "They justify their actions with promises of power, money, or something worse. To them, the ends always justify the means."

The air between them grew heavy, the enormity of the situation settling like a storm cloud overhead.

"So what do we do?" Lily asked, her voice steadier than she felt.

"We get proof," Ethan said, his tone firm. "Enough to expose Vega and whoever she's working for. Enough to stop this before it spreads beyond this hospital."

Lily straightened, determination hardening her features. "Where do we start?"

Ethan pulled a small flash drive from his pocket, holding it out to her. "This," he said. "It's encrypted data from the hospital's private server. If we can decrypt it, we'll have access to everything Vega's been hiding—communications, lab orders, maybe even direct links to her superiors."

Lily took the drive, her fingers brushing against the cool metal. "And then what?"

"Then we use it," Ethan said. "To shut them down. To make sure this pathogen doesn't leave these walls."

Lily looked up at him, her resolve clear. "I'm in."

Ethan nodded, his eyes meeting hers. "Good. But you need to be careful, Lily. Vega's dangerous, and if she knows how close we're getting, she won't hesitate to protect herself."

"She already threatened me," Lily said quietly.

Ethan's jaw clenched, his expression darkening. "Then we're out of time. We need to move fast."

As Ethan stepped back into the shadows, Lily stayed rooted in place, clutching the flash drive tightly in her hand. The cold night air bit at her skin, but she barely noticed.

The weight of what lay ahead pressed heavily on her, but so did the certainty of what needed to be done. With Ethan by her side, she knew they had a chance—however slim—to stop the unthinkable.

She turned toward the hospital, her steps steady despite the storm of emotions swirling within her. There was no turning back now. The truth was out there, buried beneath layers of lies and deceit.

And she was determined to find it.

Chapter 11
Dangerous Revelations

The ER was a cacophony of noise—blaring monitors, frantic footsteps, and the murmur of voices that carried an undercurrent of panic. Lily moved through the chaos with practiced efficiency, but tonight, something felt different. The air was charged, thick with an unspoken tension that seemed to press against her chest.

"Dr. Chen!" A nurse's voice broke through the din, sharp and urgent. "We've got another one!"

Lily spun toward the voice, her heart sinking as she saw the gurney being rushed into a nearby bay. The patient—a middle-aged man—was pale and sweating profusely, his labored breathing audible even over the noise of the ER. His vitals were displayed on the monitor, the numbers blinking dangerously low.

"What's his status?" she demanded, pulling on gloves as she approached.

"Fever of 104. Hypotensive. Respiratory distress. He collapsed at home, and his wife called EMS," the nurse rattled off, her tone clipped but tense. "Looks like the same symptoms as the others."

Lily froze for a split second, her mind racing. **It's happening again. Another infection. Another patient slipping through my fingers.** She shook off the thought, focusing on the task at hand. "Let's stabilize him. Push fluids, start broad-spectrum antibiotics, and get a respiratory panel—"

Her voice faltered as she locked eyes with the patient. He was conscious, barely, his gaze glassy and filled with a silent plea. His lips moved, forming words she couldn't hear over the noise.

"Dr. Chen?" Ethan's voice startled her. He was standing at the edge of the chaos, his sharp gaze fixed on her. "What's wrong?"

"I…" She couldn't explain it. Something about the man—his pallor, the way his chest rose and fell in shallow gasps—set off alarm bells in her mind. It wasn't just the symptoms; it was as if she could feel the infection itself, coursing through his body like an invasive force.

"Move," she ordered, stepping closer to the gurney. Her hands hovered over the patient's chest, her pulse pounding in her ears. "This isn't just respiratory failure. It's… it's deeper than that."

"Deeper?" Ethan echoed, stepping closer. "Lily, what are you—?"

"I can feel it," she interrupted, her voice trembling. "It's like… like something's wrong with his cells. They're fighting something they don't recognize."

The nurse gave her a wary glance. "Dr. Chen, should we intubate?"

"No!" Lily snapped, her voice sharper than she intended. "Not yet. Just… give me a second."

Her hands trembled as she pressed them against the man's chest, and then it happened. A rush of heat surged through her, starting in her core and spreading outward like wildfire. Her vision blurred, and for a moment, the world around her faded away. In its place, she saw something impossible—an intricate network of energy pulsing beneath the man's skin, a glowing map of his infection.

"What the hell?" she whispered, her voice barely audible.

The infection wasn't just spreading—it was attacking specific systems, exploiting weaknesses. She could see it, feel it, as if the pathogen's strategy was laid bare before her. Without thinking, she focused on the brightest point of the energy, her hands instinctively pressing down.

The patient let out a shuddering breath, his body jerking as if he'd been shocked. The glowing network pulsed once, then dimmed, the heat in Lily's hands dissipating as quickly as it had come. She staggered back, her head spinning.

"His vitals are stabilizing!" the nurse exclaimed, her voice tinged with disbelief. "Heart rate's up. O2 levels are improving."

Lily stared at her hands, her breath coming in shallow gasps. "I… I didn't do anything."

Ethan caught her arm, steadying her. "Lily, what just happened?"

"I don't know," she said, her voice trembling. "I just—he was dying, and I… I felt something. Like I knew exactly where the infection was and how to stop it."

Ethan's brow furrowed, his grip tightening slightly. "That's not normal, Lily."

She looked up at him, her eyes wide. "You think I don't know that? I don't—" She broke off, shaking her head. "It was like… I could see inside him. Not just physically, but… biologically. On a cellular level."

He studied her for a long moment, his expression unreadable. "You just saved his life."

"But how?" she whispered, her hands trembling. "Ethan, what is happening to me?"

He hesitated, then said quietly, "Maybe it's not something to fear. Maybe it's something to use."

Lily swallowed hard, her mind racing. She wasn't sure what scared her more—the fact that she had somehow tapped into something beyond her understanding, or the quiet, thrilling realization that she had done the impossible.

The patient's breathing evened out, his color returning, and Lily stepped back, her legs shaky. "This changes everything," she murmured, more to herself than to Ethan.

"It does," Ethan agreed, his voice steady. "But we'll figure it out. Together."

She nodded, her resolve hardening. Whatever was happening to her, she couldn't ignore it. Not anymore. **If this was the key to saving lives, to stopping Harlow's plan, she couldn't afford to be afraid.**

Not when the stakes were this high.

The dim glow of the ER's emergency lights cast long shadows along the corridor as Ethan stood just outside the patient's bay, his arms crossed tightly over his chest. He watched Lily with quiet intensity as she hovered near the gurney, her hands trembling faintly at her sides. The room was quieter now, the immediate crisis averted, but the tension between them was palpable.

Lily turned away from the patient, her face pale, her eyes wide with a mixture of awe and fear. She barely made it two steps before Ethan caught her by the arm, his grip firm but gentle.

"Lily," he said, his voice low and steady. "Talk to me."

"I can't," she whispered, shaking her head. Her hands still tingled with the strange warmth that had surged through her moments ago. "I don't even know where to start."

"Try," he urged, guiding her away from the bustling ER and into the quiet of an empty supply room. Once inside, he closed the door, leaning back against it. "You just saved that man's life in a way I've never seen before. You knew exactly what to do, Lily. That wasn't luck."

She crossed her arms over her chest, her voice trembling. "It wasn't medicine either. At least, not the kind I was taught."

Ethan nodded, his expression calm but probing. "Then what was it?"

She hesitated, her gaze darting to the floor. "I don't know. It's like—I could feel it, Ethan. The infection, the way it was spreading through his body. It wasn't just intuition. It was something… deeper. Something I can't explain."

He stepped closer, his tone softening. "Whatever it was, it worked. That man is alive because of you."

"But what if it wasn't supposed to happen?" she said, her voice rising with emotion. "What if this… thing, whatever it is, isn't something I can control? What if it's dangerous?"

Ethan studied her for a long moment, his gaze unwavering. "Do you think it's dangerous?"

She faltered, her arms tightening around herself. "I don't know. I mean, it didn't feel wrong, exactly. It felt like… like it was part of me, but something I didn't know was there until now."

He reached out, resting a hand on her shoulder. "And what do your instincts tell you?"

Her eyes met his, and she exhaled shakily. "That it's connected to everything happening here. To the infections, the pathogen, Harlow's experiments. It's all tied together. But if I lean into it, if I try to understand it—what if I lose control?"

"You won't," Ethan said firmly, his voice steady with conviction.

"You don't know that," she countered, frustration flickering in her tone. "I don't even know that."

"What I know," Ethan said, stepping closer, "is that your instincts have saved lives. Your patients trust you because you don't back down, even when the odds are stacked against you. This is no different."

She looked at him, her resolve wavering. "It feels different."

"Because it's new," he said gently. "And yeah, that's terrifying. But Lily, if anyone can figure out how to use this without losing themselves, it's you."

She let out a hollow laugh, brushing a hand through her hair. "You make it sound so simple."

"It's not," he admitted. "But I've seen you in action. I've seen the way you fight for your patients, the way you throw yourself into the fire for people who need you. That doesn't come from training. That comes from who you are."

Her throat tightened, and she blinked quickly, trying to push back the sudden sting of tears. "What if I'm not enough? What if this… whatever it is, isn't enough to stop what's coming?"

Ethan's hand shifted to cup her cheek, his touch grounding her. "Then we fight anyway. Because that's who we are."

The sincerity in his voice broke something inside her, and she exhaled shakily, leaning into his touch for just a moment. "I'm scared, Ethan. Of what this means, of what I might become."

He nodded, his gaze unwavering. "I know. But you don't have to face it alone. I trust you, Lily—more than anyone else I've ever worked with. And if this is part of who you are, then I trust that too."

Her breath hitched, and she stepped back, her resolve hardening as she looked at him. "Thank you," she said softly. "For… not running."

"Never crossed my mind," he said with a faint smile.

She allowed herself a small, determined smile in return. "Then let's figure out what this means. And how we use it to stop Harlow."

Ethan nodded, his expression serious but warm. "Together."

As they left the supply room, their bond felt stronger than ever, forged in the heat of their shared mission and the vulnerability they had allowed themselves to show. Whatever lay ahead, they knew they could face it—together.

The quiet hum of the ER faded into the background as Lily stood by the sink in the staff restroom, gripping the edge of the counter. She stared at her reflection in the mirror, her face pale, her eyes clouded with a storm of emotions. The memory of the surge—the warmth, the light, the undeniable connection to something greater than herself—played on a loop in her mind.

She didn't flinch when the door creaked open, and Ethan stepped inside, his expression cautious but unwavering.

"Didn't think I'd find you hiding," he said, leaning casually against the doorframe.

"I'm not hiding," she muttered, though her tight grip on the counter betrayed her nerves. "I just needed a minute."

"Well, you've had a few," he said, his tone light but firm. "Time's up."

She let out a frustrated sigh, turning to face him. "I'm trying to wrap my head around what just happened, Ethan. I'm not sure a 'minute' is enough for that."

He nodded, stepping closer. "Fair. But while you're in here spinning out, the world out there isn't slowing down. Harlow isn't slowing down."

Her shoulders sagged slightly, and she turned back to the mirror. "I don't even know what I am anymore," she said quietly. "A doctor? Some… experiment gone wrong? A freak?"

"Stop," Ethan said sharply, his voice cutting through her spiraling thoughts. "You're not a freak, Lily."

She glared at him through the mirror, her voice rising. "Then what am I? Because I sure as hell don't feel normal. Normal doctors don't see infections glowing under a patient's skin. They don't—"

"Save lives the way you just did?" he interrupted, stepping even closer. "Normal doctors don't do what you do, Lily, powers or not."

She shook her head, her hands curling into fists. "I didn't sign up for this. I signed up to help people, to heal them. Not to… to become some kind of weapon."

Ethan's voice softened, though it carried the weight of conviction. "And you are helping people. You're healing them in ways no one else can. You think Harlow's playing by the rules? You think the people funding him care about normal?"

Her eyes locked with his, and her voice faltered. "What if I can't control it? What if I hurt someone?"

"You won't," he said simply. "Because that's not who you are."

She scoffed, turning away from him. "You have way too much faith in me, Ethan."

"Maybe," he said, his voice steady, "but I'm not wrong. You've been fighting this since the moment we uncovered it. You didn't back down when you saw what Harlow was capable of.

You didn't quit when Caleb betrayed us. And you sure as hell didn't quit when you realized this fight was bigger than just the hospital."

Her breath hitched, and she blinked quickly, willing the tears away. "It's different now. If I accept this—if I use these powers—I'm crossing a line I can't uncross."

"And maybe that's exactly what needs to happen," he said, his gaze unwavering. "This isn't just about Harlow anymore, Lily. It's about everyone he's put at risk—everyone who doesn't even know they're in danger. You have the power to stop this. To save lives. But you have to choose to use it."

She turned to him fully, her chest tight with the weight of his words. "What if I'm not enough? What if I fail?"

Ethan stepped closer, his voice quiet but resolute. "You won't. Because you're not doing this alone. I'm with you every step of the way."

Her throat tightened, and she exhaled shakily. "It's a lot, Ethan. The responsibility, the risk. It's… overwhelming."

"I know," he said, his tone softening. "But you're not the kind of person who runs from responsibility. You step into it. That's what makes you you."

She stared at him, the storm inside her beginning to calm. Slowly, she nodded, her resolve hardening. "You're right. This isn't about me anymore. It's about stopping Harlow, protecting the people he's put in danger."

Ethan's lips curved into the faintest of smiles. "So, what's next, Doc?"

She straightened, her gaze steady. "We go after Shaw. We get the rest of the puzzle and use it to take Harlow down. And I stop being afraid of what I can do."

"Good," he said, his voice firm. "Because we're going to need all the help we can get."

As they left the restroom, the tension between them shifted, replaced by a quiet but powerful sense of unity. Lily felt the weight of her responsibility pressing down on her, but it no longer felt paralyzing. It felt empowering.

Whatever she was, whatever these powers meant, she would use them to fight for the truth—and to stop the catastrophe looming on the horizon. She wasn't running anymore. She was ready to face it head-on.

The small conference room was quiet except for the faint hum of the overhead lights. The stark, sterile environment felt out of place given the gravity of the moment. Ethan leaned against the table, his arms crossed, while Lily stood near the whiteboard, pacing as her thoughts poured out in fragments.

"Shaw's the linchpin," she said, her voice steady despite the tension in her tone. "If we can catch him, get him to talk, we'll have enough to bring Harlow down."

Ethan nodded, his sharp eyes following her movements. "And if he doesn't talk?"

"He will," she said firmly, stopping mid-step to look at him. "We'll make him."

Ethan raised an eyebrow, his lips curving into a faint smile. "You're more intimidating than you give yourself credit for, Doc."

She let out a soft laugh, the sound tinged with exhaustion. "I'll take that as a compliment."

"It was," he said, his expression softening. "But let's say Shaw's not the weak link we're hoping for. What's plan B?"

Lily sighed, rubbing the back of her neck. "Plan B is getting enough evidence from the lab to expose Harlow without Shaw's cooperation. Those logs, the supply records, the patient files—they're all pieces of the puzzle."

"And Harlow's been covering his tracks," Ethan pointed out. "The deeper we dig, the more dangerous it gets."

She met his gaze, her resolve hardening. "I know. But we don't have a choice. If we don't stop him now, more people will die."

Ethan pushed off the table, stepping closer. "And what happens when we confront him? You think he's just going to roll over and confess?"

"No," she admitted, her voice quieter now. "But we're not walking into this blind. We'll have the evidence, and we'll have each other."

He tilted his head slightly, studying her. "You've changed."

"What?" she asked, caught off guard.

"You," he said, his tone thoughtful. "You're not the same doctor who walked into that ER a few months ago, wide-eyed and determined to save the world."

Her lips twitched into a faint smile. "And who am I now?"

"You're someone who's willing to fight for it," he said simply. "Even when the odds are stacked against you."

She let his words sink in, her chest tightening with a mix of pride and vulnerability. "I don't know if I could've done this without you," she said softly.

"You would've," he said, his voice steady. "But I'm glad you didn't have to."

The moment hung between them, charged and unspoken, until Lily broke the silence. "So, what's our next move?"

Ethan leaned against the edge of the table, his gaze sharp. "We go after Shaw. But we do it smart. We need a location where we can isolate him, keep things controlled."

"The supply wing," Lily suggested. "It's quiet at night, and he's been signing out samples from there. If we time it right, we can catch him in the act."

Ethan nodded, a faint smile playing on his lips. "Not bad, Doc. And what about Harlow?"

Her expression darkened. "Once we have Shaw, we go straight to Harlow. Confront him with the evidence and make it clear there's no way out."

Ethan's smile faded, replaced by a serious look. "You know he won't go down without a fight."

She crossed her arms, her jaw tightening. "I'm counting on it."

He stepped closer, his voice dropping slightly. "You're ready for this?"

"As ready as I'll ever be," she said, her eyes meeting his. "What about you?"

"I was born for this," he said with a faint smirk, though his eyes betrayed the weight of what lay ahead. "But this isn't just my fight anymore. It's ours."

Her chest tightened at the quiet intensity of his words. "Then we finish it. Together."

He nodded, his expression softening. "Together."

The room fell into a comfortable silence, their shared resolve anchoring them in the face of uncertainty. Whatever came next, they knew they couldn't turn back now. The fight wasn't just about Harlow, or Shaw, or even the hospital—it was about standing up against something bigger, something darker.

"Lily," Ethan said after a moment, his tone quieter now. "Whatever happens out there, I need you to know—I trust you. Completely."

Her breath caught, and she nodded, her voice soft but firm. "I trust you too, Ethan. More than anyone."

The weight of their shared mission settled over them as they prepared to step into the storm. Their fate was uncertain, but their bond was unshakable. Together, they would face whatever came next—no matter the cost.

Chapter 12
Ethical Crossroads

The staff lounge was quiet except for the sputtering of the coffee machine as it dispensed another weak brew into Lily's cup. She leaned against the counter, staring blankly at the swirling liquid, her mind far from the mundane motions of brewing coffee.

The door swung open, and Nina stepped inside, her sharp gaze immediately locking onto Lily. "You look like you've just gone twelve rounds with a hurricane," Nina said, crossing her arms as she leaned against the counter beside her. "What's going on, rookie?"

"Just… a lot on my plate," Lily replied, forcing a smile that felt as weak as the coffee she was holding.

Nina raised an eyebrow, clearly unconvinced. "You're a terrible liar, Chen. Spill."

Lily hesitated, her fingers tightening around the cup. "It's nothing, really. Just the usual stress. Patients crashing, cases piling up, that kind of thing."

"The usual stress doesn't make you stare at a coffee machine like it just insulted your mother," Nina shot back, her tone blunt but not unkind. "Whatever it is, don't let it eat you alive. You're no good to anyone if you're a wreck."

Lily managed a soft chuckle, but it faded quickly. "Thanks for the pep talk, Coach."

"Anytime," Nina said, her eyes narrowing slightly as she studied Lily. "Seriously, though, if you need to talk, you know where to find me."

Lily nodded, grateful for the offer but knowing she couldn't take Nina up on it—not this time. As Nina left the room, Lily's thoughts spiraled back to the patient who had crashed earlier, the sound of the flatline still ringing in her ears. Another life hanging by a thread, another case with too many unanswered questions.

Ethan's voice echoed in her mind, low and urgent: *This goes deeper than you think.*

Her stomach churned, and she set the coffee down on the counter. She couldn't drink it. She couldn't even think straight.

The door opened again, this time revealing Ethan. His expression was unreadable, but his presence alone was enough to make her pulse quicken.

"You're a hard woman to find," he said, his tone lighter than the look in his eyes.

Lily folded her arms, leaning back against the counter. "What do you want, Ethan?"

He stepped closer, his voice dropping. "You. To be honest with me."

"About what?"

"You're hesitating," he said, his gaze piercing. "I can see it all over your face. You've got doubts about what we're doing."

Lily frowned, her heart racing. "It's not that simple. This isn't black and white, Ethan. These are people's lives we're dealing with."

"And that's exactly why we're doing this," he replied firmly. "To save lives. To stop this before it spreads."

"But at what cost?" Lily shot back. "If we're wrong—if we accuse the wrong person or make the wrong move—how many people get hurt because of us?"

Ethan held her gaze, his expression softening slightly. "I get it," he said quietly. "This isn't easy. It's not supposed to be. But you can't let the what-ifs paralyze you. You're too smart for that."

"It's not about being smart," Lily said, her voice trembling. "It's about being responsible. I've seen what happens when doctors overstep. The damage it does. The lives it ruins."

"And what about the lives you save?" Ethan countered. "Because that's what this is about, Lily. Saving lives. Stopping this before it's too late."

Lily looked away, her chest tightening. "I just… I don't know if I'm strong enough for this."

Ethan stepped closer, his voice soft but steady. "You are. You wouldn't be here if you weren't."

She met his gaze again, her doubts still swirling but tempered by the determination in his eyes. "What if I fail?"

"Then we fail together," Ethan said. "But if we don't try, we've already lost."

The weight of his words settled over her, heavy but grounding. She nodded slowly, the tension in her chest easing just enough to let her breathe.

"Alright," she said quietly. "I'm in."

Ethan's lips curved into a faint smile. "That's what I wanted to hear."

As he turned to leave, Lily stayed where she was, the faint hum of the coffee machine filling the silence. The weight of her decision still loomed, but for the first time, it didn't feel crushing. It felt purposeful.

She picked up her cup again, taking a tentative sip. It was bitter, almost undrinkable, but it was enough to steady her nerves. For now, that would have to be enough.

The soft hum of fluorescent lights filled the air in the quiet corner of the hospital, where Lily and Ethan sat huddled over a laptop. The room was small, tucked away from the bustling ER, with only the faint sounds of footsteps and distant voices filtering through the closed door.

“These lab results don’t match up,” Lily said, her brow furrowed as she pointed to the screen. “Look—same patient, but two different sets of data. Bloodwork run on the same day, but the results are completely inconsistent.”

Ethan leaned in, his sharp gaze scanning the screen. “Deliberate,” he muttered, his voice low. “Someone’s falsifying records to cover their tracks.”

Lily shook her head, the frustration evident in her voice. “Why go through all this trouble? What are they hiding?”

Ethan straightened, his jaw tightening. “Whatever it is, it’s big enough for them to risk everything. You don’t falsify medical records unless you’ve got something to lose.”

Lily sat back, her arms crossed. “So what’s the next step? How do we prove it?”

Ethan hesitated for a moment, his usual confidence giving way to something quieter, more thoughtful. “We keep looking,” he said finally. “Patterns, inconsistencies, anything that ties back to Vega or her superiors. The more we find, the harder it’ll be for them to explain it away.”

As they worked, the silence between them was punctuated by the soft clicks of the keyboard and the faint rustle of papers. Lily’s focus was razor-sharp, her eyes darting across the screen as she pieced together the fragments of data.

Then Ethan spoke, his voice quieter than usual. “You know, this isn’t the first time I’ve seen something like this.”

Lily glanced at him, her curiosity piqued. "What do you mean?"

Ethan leaned back in his chair, his gaze distant. "A few years ago, I was part of an operation overseas. We were tracking a similar kind of setup—bioweapons, cover-ups, the works. We got close, real close. But…" He paused, his expression darkening.

"But what?" Lily prompted gently.

Ethan's jaw tightened, and he exhaled sharply. "We lost someone. A teammate. My fault."

Lily frowned, her chest tightening at the weight in his voice. "Ethan, I'm sure it wasn't—"

"It was," he interrupted, his tone firm but not unkind. "I made a call. Took a risk. And it cost her life. I've carried that with me ever since."

The room fell into a heavy silence, the hum of the laptop the only sound.

"I can't let this happen again," Ethan said finally, his voice low but steady. "Not here. Not with you."

Lily studied him for a moment, the vulnerability in his words striking a chord deep within her. Despite his guarded exterior, there was a pain there, a drive that mirrored her own.

"Then we won't," she said firmly, her voice cutting through the quiet. "We're going to figure this out, Ethan. And we're going to stop it."

Ethan's lips curved into a faint smile, the tension in his expression easing slightly. "I believe you, Doc."

The weight in the room shifted, the shared determination between them igniting a spark of hope. As they turned back to the laptop, the data before them felt less like an insurmountable puzzle and more like a challenge they were ready to face together.

Lily tapped the screen again, her voice gaining momentum. "Look at this—another patient with discrepancies. Same pattern, same delays in reporting. If we cross-reference these with the lab requisitions…"

Ethan nodded, his focus sharpening. "We can start connecting the dots. And once we have a clear trail…"

"We take it to someone who can't ignore it," Lily finished, her resolve hardening.

Ethan met her gaze, his eyes gleaming with determination. "Exactly."

As they worked late into the night, the quiet corner of the hospital became their war room, the pieces of the case slowly falling into place. For the first time, the overwhelming uncertainty began to give way to clarity. They were on the right track, and nothing was going to stop them now.

The hospital was cloaked in an uneasy silence late that night, the usual hum of activity replaced by the occasional distant echo of footsteps. Lily's heart pounded in her chest as she stood at the edge of the corridor, her eyes locked on the figure slipping through the double doors marked *Infectious Disease Wing – Restricted Access.*

Dr. Vega.

Her breath quickened as she waited for the doors to close before following at a distance. The hallway felt colder here, the fluorescent lights casting long, sharp shadows. Lily moved carefully, keeping close to the wall as she approached the doors. They were slightly ajar, just enough for her to see inside.

Vega stood near a workstation, her posture tense. Across from her was a man Lily didn't recognize—a tall figure in a dark suit, his presence unsettling in the sterile hospital setting.

"We're too exposed," Vega hissed, her voice sharp but low.

The man's response was equally cutting. "Finish the work," he said, his tone as smooth as it was threatening. "Or we'll find someone who will."

Lily's breath caught, her pulse roaring in her ears. The exchange sent a chill down her spine. This wasn't just a mistake or negligence—this was deliberate.

Vega’s head snapped toward the door, and Lily froze. For a moment, she thought she was hidden, but then Vega’s eyes locked onto hers.

“Dr. Chen,” Vega said, her tone icy as she stepped toward the door. “What are you doing here?”

Lily’s mouth went dry, her mind scrambling for an answer. “I—”

Before she could speak, a shadow moved behind her. Ethan.

“She’s with me,” Ethan said, his voice steady but hard as he stepped forward. His presence was commanding, and for a moment, Lily felt a surge of relief.

Vega’s lips curled into a sneer, her composure slipping just enough to reveal the anger simmering beneath. “Careful, Dr. Chen,” she said, her voice dripping with venom. “You don’t want to get involved in things you can’t handle.”

“And what exactly would those be?” Ethan asked, his tone challenging as he moved between Lily and Vega.

Vega’s gaze flicked between them, her eyes narrowing. “You think you’re clever, don’t you?” she said, her words aimed at Ethan. “But cleverness doesn’t mean anything when you’re out of your depth.”

“Funny,” Ethan replied, his smirk faint but deliberate. “I was just about to say the same thing to you.”

Vega's jaw tightened, and for a moment, Lily thought she might lash out. But instead, Vega straightened, smoothing her coat with a calculated motion. "This isn't over," she said coldly, her gaze lingering on Lily. "Not for any of us."

With that, Vega turned and disappeared down the corridor, the sound of her heels echoing against the tile.

Lily exhaled shakily, her legs threatening to give out beneath her. "She knows," she whispered, her voice barely audible.

"She's known for a while," Ethan said, his tone grim as he placed a steadying hand on her shoulder. "But now she's worried. That's good—it means we're getting closer."

Lily shook her head, the tension in her chest threatening to overwhelm her. "What if she's right? What if we're in over our heads?"

Ethan's grip on her shoulder tightened slightly, his voice firm but reassuring. "We're not," he said. "Not as long as we stay ahead of her. You saw her back there—she's scared. That's when people like her make mistakes."

Lily nodded slowly, his words grounding her just enough to catch her breath. "What do we do now?"

"We keep building the case," Ethan said. "But you need to be careful, Lily. Vega's not bluffing—she'll do whatever it takes to protect herself."

Lily looked at him, her fear giving way to resolve. "So will we," she said quietly.

Ethan's lips curved into a faint smile, his respect for her determination evident. "That's the spirit."

As they turned to leave, Lily glanced back at the doors to the Infectious Disease Wing, the weight of what she had overheard settling heavily on her shoulders. The stakes had never been higher, and the line between right and wrong had never felt so thin.

But she knew one thing for certain—she couldn't turn back now.

The makeshift base Ethan had set up in an unused hospital storage room was cluttered but functional. Laptops, files, and scattered notes covered a metal table in the center of the room, the dim lighting casting long shadows on the walls. Lily paced back and forth, her mind racing as Ethan sat at the table, typing rapidly on a laptop.

"We need irrefutable proof," Ethan said, his tone firm as he gestured to the screen. "Something concrete we can take to the authorities. If we don't have that, they'll bury this, and Vega will walk away clean."

Lily stopped pacing and turned to face him. "What kind of proof are we talking about?"

"Communications, financial trails, orders directly linking her to the pathogen and whoever she's working for," Ethan replied. "Something they can't explain away as a clerical error or bad judgment."

She nodded, her earlier fear now hardened into resolve. "Then let's find it."

Ethan glanced up at her, his gaze softening. "Are you sure about this?" he asked quietly. "Once we do this, there's no going back. Not for you, not for your career, and maybe not for your safety."

"There was no going back the moment I saw those patients," Lily said, her voice steady. "They trusted us to help them, and we let them down. I won't let it happen again."

Ethan studied her for a long moment, his usual guarded expression giving way to something closer to admiration. "Alright," he said finally, his tone laced with respect. "Let's finish this."

He turned back to the laptop, his fingers flying over the keys as he brought up a map of the hospital's network. "The files we need are on the internal server Vega's been using to manipulate the records. It's heavily encrypted, but I can bypass it."

"How long will it take?" Lily asked, stepping closer to peer at the screen.

"Depends on how deep they've buried it," Ethan replied. "But once we're in, we need to move fast. If Vega catches wind of this, she'll destroy everything before we can use it."

Lily nodded, her heart pounding. "What do you need me to do?"

"Keep watch," Ethan said without looking up. "If Vega or anyone else shows up, I need time to finish this."

She moved to the door, her nerves taut as she kept an ear out for approaching footsteps. The silence outside the room was unnerving, each creak and shuffle amplified in her mind.

Minutes stretched into what felt like hours as Ethan worked, his face illuminated by the glow of the screen. The tension in the room was palpable, every second ticking by with the weight of what they were risking.

"Got it," Ethan said finally, his voice breaking the silence.

Lily turned quickly. "You found it?"

He nodded, spinning the laptop to face her. "Everything. Financial transactions tied to offshore accounts, emails ordering the disposal of patient samples, even direct communications with her superiors."

Lily stared at the screen, her chest tightening as the pieces fell into place. "This is enough to take her down."

"More than enough," Ethan said, his tone grim. "But we need to act fast. If she finds out we have this…"

"She won't," Lily interrupted, her resolve firm. "We'll take this to someone who can stop her. Someone who can't be silenced."

Ethan's gaze lingered on her, a faint smile tugging at the corner of his lips. "You're tougher than you look, Doc."

"And you're not as cynical as you pretend to be," she shot back, a small smile breaking through her tension.

He chuckled softly, the sound brief but genuine. "Let's get to work."

As they began transferring the files to a secure drive, the reality of what they were about to do loomed large. The risks were immense, but so were the stakes.

Lily glanced at Ethan, her determination mirrored in his expression. "No matter what happens," she said quietly, "thank you. For trusting me."

Ethan nodded, his voice steady. "We're in this together."

The night stretched on, the hum of the laptop and the distant echoes of the hospital the only sounds. They were on the brink of exposing the truth, and there was no turning back now. Together, they prepared for the final push, ready to face whatever came next.

Chapter 13
The Walls Close In

The air in the lab felt heavier now, as though the room itself sensed the danger brewing within. Lily and Ethan stood near the entrance, their presence sharp and commanding despite the tension that hummed in the sterile space. Across from them, Dr. Harlow leaned casually against the counter, his white coat pristine, his expression calm. Markus Shaw, less composed, hovered near the refrigeration unit, his hands twitching at his sides.

"I was wondering when you two would show up," Harlow said smoothly, his voice carrying the weight of a man who believed himself untouchable. "I have to admit, your persistence is impressive."

Lily's jaw tightened, the manifest she carried crinkling under her grip. "It's over, Harlow. We have enough evidence to expose everything—your experiments, your transport plans, the pathogen itself."

Harlow raised an eyebrow, a faint smile curving his lips. "Evidence? Oh, Dr. Chen, you're smarter than that. Evidence can be… interpreted. Misunderstood. Buried."

Ethan stepped forward, his stance rigid, his voice low and dangerous. "Not this time. We've got records, photos, patient files—all pointing directly to you. You can't explain this away."

Harlow chuckled softly, shaking his head. "And what exactly do you think you're accomplishing? Disrupting a project that could save humanity? That's short-sighted, even for you, Dr. Chen."

Lily's eyes narrowed, her voice steady despite the chill that crept into her chest. "You're killing people, Harlow. Innocent people. You're using them like lab rats."

"Progress demands sacrifice," Harlow replied, his tone maddeningly calm. "Do you think the great leaps in science were achieved without casualties? Without hard choices? What I'm doing here—what *we* are doing—will redefine what it means to be human."

Ethan's fists clenched at his sides. "By unleashing a pathogen on an entire city? That's not progress—that's genocide."

"Genocide?" Harlow repeated, his tone almost amused. "No, no. You misunderstand. This isn't about death—it's about control. Imagine a world where illness could be eradicated, where immunity could be tailored to the individual. The pathogen is just a means to an end."

Lily's stomach twisted as his words settled over her, the depth of his delusion chilling her to the bone. "And what about the lives you're destroying in the process? The families you're tearing apart?"

Harlow's gaze sharpened, his smile fading. "Sacrifices, Dr. Chen. Necessary sacrifices. Do you think you're any different? How many patients have you lost in surgery? How many lives have slipped through your fingers because you weren't good enough?"

Her breath caught, but Ethan stepped in, his voice cutting through the room like a blade. "Enough. You're not some visionary, Harlow. You're a coward. Hiding behind science to justify your greed and your ego."

Harlow's eyes flicked to Ethan, his expression darkening. "And you, Mr. Wilde. The soldier turned hero. Tell me, how many people have you killed in the name of duty? How many lives have you deemed expendable for the greater good?"

Ethan didn't flinch, his gaze locked with Harlow's. "None of that justifies what you're doing here. This ends tonight."

Shaw, who had been silent until now, shifted uneasily, his voice breaking the tense standoff. "Dr. Harlow, maybe we should—"

"Quiet," Harlow snapped, his voice cold. "You've done your part, Markus. Stay out of this."

Lily's gaze darted to Shaw, noting the flicker of fear in his eyes. "You don't have to keep doing this, Shaw. Harlow's using you. You're a loose end to him."

Shaw hesitated, his hands trembling. "I didn't sign up for this. I thought… I thought we were helping people."

"You still can," Lily urged, her tone softening. "Help us stop this before it's too late."

"Enough," Harlow barked, his calm veneer cracking. He stepped forward, his eyes blazing with fury. "You think you can walk in here, throw around accusations, and win? You have no idea what you're up against."

Lily squared her shoulders, her voice steady. "We know exactly what we're up against. And we're not afraid of you."

Harlow smiled again, but it was cold, devoid of humor. "You should be. Because if you think you've won, you're gravely mistaken."

The tension in the room crackled like a live wire, the unspoken threat hanging heavy in the air. Lily's heart pounded, but she refused to waver. Whatever came next, she and Ethan would face it together. This was the moment they had been racing toward—a confrontation that would decide the fate of everyone Harlow had endangered.

And they weren't backing down. Not now. Not ever.

The tension in the lab exploded like a coiled spring. Harlow's face twisted with fury as he barked an order to his hidden team. From a concealed door, two men in dark uniforms surged into the room, their movements sharp and efficient. Ethan's stance shifted instantly, his hand darting to his side as he stepped in front of Lily.

"Stay behind me," he commanded, his voice low and steady.

"Ethan—" Lily began, her voice trembling.

"Now, Lily," he snapped, not taking his eyes off the approaching men.

The first blow came fast—a brutal swing aimed at Ethan's head. He ducked smoothly, his counterstrike landing squarely in the man's ribs. The second man lunged, but Ethan twisted, using the momentum to throw him into the nearest counter. Equipment clattered to the ground, the sharp sound echoing through the sterile lab.

Harlow's voice cut through the chaos, cold and commanding. "Don't let them leave this room. Secure the samples."

Lily's heart pounded as she scrambled to the far side of the lab, her mind racing. Her eyes darted to the refrigeration unit—Harlow's prized repository of the pathogen. If she could disable it, she could at least buy them time.

"Lily, what are you doing?" Ethan's voice reached her between the grunts of effort as he engaged the two men.

"Stopping this!" she shouted, grabbing a nearby metal tray and jamming it into the base of the refrigeration unit. Sparks erupted as the tray wedged itself into the exposed wiring. The humming of the unit faltered, then stopped.

Harlow's attention snapped to her, his expression a mix of fury and disbelief. "Do you have any idea what you've done?"

"I know exactly what I've done," she shot back, her voice steady despite her shaking hands. "You're not using this pathogen to hurt anyone else."

Harlow lunged toward her, but Ethan intercepted him, shoving him back with a force that sent him stumbling into a counter. "Not so fast," Ethan growled. He turned just in time to block another strike from one of Harlow's men, his movements precise and efficient despite the chaos around him.

Lily darted to another workstation, searching for anything she could use to keep sabotaging Harlow's operation. Her eyes landed on a set of syringes filled with clear liquid—likely part of the pathogen's stabilizing formula. She grabbed them, her breath hitching as Harlow straightened, his face a mask of rage.

"Enough of this," Harlow snarled, his voice sharp and cutting. "You don't understand what you're meddling with."

"Oh, I understand perfectly," Lily said, holding up the syringes. "You've been playing God, and now it's over."

Harlow's gaze flickered to the syringes, a brief flash of panic breaking through his composure. "Put those down, Dr. Chen."

"Or what?" she challenged, her grip tightening on the syringes.

"Lily, heads up!" Ethan's voice called out as one of the men lunged at her. She barely ducked in time, the movement throwing her off balance. The syringes clattered to the floor, skittering under a counter.

The man who had lunged at her turned, ready to strike again, but Ethan was faster. He slammed the man into the wall with a force that left him crumpling to the ground. Breathing heavily, Ethan glanced at Lily, his voice sharp with concern. "You okay?"

"Fine," she managed, her heart racing. "But we need to destroy what's left."

He nodded, his gaze flicking to the refrigeration unit. "That's the priority. Can you handle it?"

She hesitated for a fraction of a second, then nodded. "I'll finish it."

Ethan turned back to face the remaining threats, his movements fluid and calculated as he disarmed the second man. Harlow, seeing the tide turning, lunged for the syringes under the counter, but Lily was faster. She slid across the floor, kicking them out of his reach and sending them smashing against the wall.

"No!" Harlow roared, his composure fracturing completely. He lunged at Lily, his hands reaching for her throat.

Ethan was there in an instant, pulling Harlow off her and pinning him against the counter. "You're done, Harlow," he growled, his voice low and dangerous.

Harlow sneered, his voice venomous. "You think you've won? You're too late. The release is already set."

Lily scrambled to her feet, her voice sharp. "Not if I can stop it."

She raced to the central terminal, her hands flying over the keyboard as she searched for the release protocol. The screen flashed red—**Release Imminent.**

"Ethan!" she shouted, panic edging into her voice.

"Do what you need to do," he called back, still holding Harlow in place. "I've got him."

Her fingers moved faster, bypassing security measures and canceling commands. The countdown on the screen slowed, then froze.

"Got it," she breathed, relief flooding her. "It's stopped."

Ethan glanced at her, a small, fierce smile breaking through his tension. "Nice work, Doc."

But as the chaos quieted, Lily knew it wasn't over yet. Harlow's twisted vision had brought them here, but the fight to stop him completely was far from finished. The weight of their victory hung precariously, and the cost of failure loomed over them like a shadow.

The lab was chaos incarnate. Equipment lay shattered on the floor, the refrigeration unit smoldering from Lily's earlier sabotage. Harlow's henchman—the last one standing—was relentless, his movements quick and brutal. Ethan squared off with him, his stance defensive but unwavering as the man lunged forward with a sharp metal rod he'd salvaged from the wreckage.

"Lily, stay back!" Ethan shouted, his voice tight with effort as he blocked another swing.

"I'm trying!" she shot back, furiously typing at the central terminal to lock Harlow out of the system completely. Sweat dripped down her temple, her mind racing to stay one step ahead.

Ethan deflected the rod again, but the man twisted, landing a sharp blow to Ethan's side. He grunted in pain, staggering slightly before regaining his balance. His knuckles were white as he gripped the edge of the counter to steady himself.

"Ethan!" Lily's head snapped toward him, panic flooding her voice.

"I'm fine," he growled through clenched teeth, his jaw tightening as he squared up again. "Finish what you're doing, Doc."

But the sheen of sweat on his brow and the way he favored his side told a different story. Lily's heart clenched as she forced herself to refocus on the terminal. **If she didn't stop the release now, none of this would matter.**

The henchman pressed his advantage, delivering another strike that forced Ethan to his knees. He swung upward, catching the man's wrist and twisting it sharply. The rod clattered to the ground, but the victory was short-lived. The man drove a knee into Ethan's ribs, and Ethan crumpled with a muffled cry.

"No!" Lily shouted, abandoning the terminal as she rushed toward them. Her instincts overrode her fear as she grabbed a piece of broken equipment—a jagged metal shard—and hurled it at the henchman. It struck his arm, drawing a sharp yell of pain and forcing him to back off.

She dropped to Ethan's side, her hands trembling as they hovered over him. "Ethan, talk to me."

He coughed, wincing as he tried to sit up. "I'm fine," he rasped, his voice strained. "Just… got the wind knocked out of me."

"Liar," she said, her voice thick with emotion. Her fingers brushed against his side, and he flinched. Blood seeped through his shirt, staining her hands. "You're bleeding."

"It's nothing," he insisted, his hand weakly covering hers. "Focus on the mission, Lily. Finish it."

Her throat tightened, her vision blurring with unshed tears. "Not without you."

"You don't have a choice," he said, his gaze locking with hers. His voice softened, even as pain lined his features. "You have to stop him. Promise me."

She shook her head, her lips trembling. "Don't ask me to do that."

"I'm not asking," he said firmly. "You're the only one who can end this. You've got the strength, Lily. I've seen it."

His words lit something inside her—a fierce, blazing determination that burned through her fear. She nodded, her hands steadying as she gently pushed him back. "Stay down. I'll handle this."

He gave her a faint smile, his voice barely above a whisper. "Knew I could count on you."

Rising to her feet, Lily turned to face the henchman, who was already advancing again, his injured arm hanging awkwardly at his side. Her body hummed with adrenaline, her mind razor-sharp. **No more hesitation. No more fear.**

"You picked the wrong side," she said, her voice cold and cutting. Her grip tightened on the broken metal shard as she stepped forward, meeting him head-on.

The man lunged, but Lily moved faster, sidestepping his attack and slamming the shard into his shoulder. He stumbled, and she didn't give him a chance to recover. Using every ounce of strength she had, she drove her knee into his stomach, sending him sprawling to the floor.

"Stay down," she warned, her voice shaking with barely restrained fury.

The man groaned, clutching his shoulder as he struggled to push himself up. Before he could fully rise, Ethan's voice cut through the tension, low but resolute. "She said, stay down."

Lily glanced over her shoulder to see Ethan leaning heavily against the counter, his face pale but determined. Despite his injury, he'd managed to pull himself upright, his hand gripping a fallen metal rod.

The henchman hesitated, his eyes darting between Lily and Ethan before finally slumping back onto the floor. He didn't have the strength—or the will—to fight anymore.

Lily exhaled shakily, her anger dissipating as the reality of the moment hit her. She rushed back to Ethan, wrapping an arm around his waist to steady him. "You're insane, you know that?"

He gave her a weak smirk, his voice rough. "Takes one to know one."

Her lips quirked into a faint smile, but the worry in her eyes didn't fade. "You're lucky I'm a doctor."

"And you're lucky I'm too stubborn to quit," he countered, leaning into her for support. "Now, finish this, Doc. Let's make it count."

She nodded, her resolve hardening as she turned back to the terminal. The fight wasn't over yet, but with Ethan by her side—even injured—she felt unstoppable. Together, they would see this through to the end. **No matter what it took.**

The lab felt like it was collapsing in on itself. The alarms blared, red lights flashing across the room in chaotic bursts. Smoke billowed from the damaged refrigeration unit, and the faint hiss of gas escaping filled the air with an acrid tang. Ethan slumped against the counter, one hand pressed to his side, his breaths shallow but steady. Lily stood in the center of the chaos, her eyes locked on the terminal as the screen flickered with warnings.

Pathogen release imminent. Containment compromised.

"No," Lily whispered, her voice trembling as her fingers flew over the keys. "No, no, no. I stopped it. I—"

"It's the backup system," Ethan said, his voice rough but urgent. "Harlow must've set it to trigger automatically."

Lily's chest tightened, her breath coming in short, sharp bursts. "We can't let it spread. If this thing gets out…"

"It won't," Ethan said firmly, though his pale complexion and weakened posture betrayed his pain. "We'll stop it. Together."

She shook her head, the weight of the moment crashing down on her. "There's no time, Ethan. I can feel it—it's already in the air."

"What do you mean you can feel it?" he asked, his voice sharp with concern.

Lily's gaze darted to him, her throat tightening. "It's… I don't know how to explain it. It's like I can sense the pathogen moving, like I know where it's spreading."

"Your biomancy," Ethan said, realization dawning in his eyes. "Lily, if you can sense it, can you—?"

"I don't know!" she snapped, her voice breaking. "I've never done anything like this before. What if I make it worse?"

Ethan pushed off the counter, grimacing as he took a shaky step toward her. "And what if you stop it? You've already saved lives with your abilities, Lily. You can do this."

She stared at him, her heart pounding. "And what if it kills me?"

He reached out, his hand brushing her arm. "Then we figure it out. But if you don't try, we know what happens. You're the only one who can stop this, Lily."

Her chest tightened, her fear warring with her determination. She glanced at the room, the smoke swirling with an eerie, almost tangible presence. The pathogen felt alive, a malevolent force threatening to consume everything.

She took a deep breath, her voice trembling. "Okay. But you have to promise me something."

"Anything," Ethan said, his gaze steady.

"If this doesn't work—if I don't make it—" Her voice broke, but she forced herself to continue. "Promise me you'll stop Harlow. Promise me this won't be for nothing."

Ethan's jaw tightened, his voice low and fierce. "You're not dying, Lily. Not here. Not now."

Tears pricked at her eyes, but she nodded, drawing strength from his unwavering belief in her. She stepped to the center of the room, her body tense, her mind racing as she focused on the pathogen's presence. Closing her eyes, she reached out—not with her hands, but with something deeper, something innate.

The sensation hit her like a tidal wave. She gasped as she felt the pathogen coursing through the air, invading every particle around her. It was chaotic and relentless, but beneath the chaos, she sensed a rhythm—a pattern. She latched onto it, her mind honing in on the source.

"Lily?" Ethan's voice cut through the haze. "What's happening?"

"I can feel it," she said, her voice tight. "It's everywhere, but it's… connected. If I can disrupt the way it spreads, I might be able to contain it."

Her hands trembled as she extended them, her body vibrating with energy she didn't fully understand. Heat surged through her veins, a blazing fire that threatened to consume her. She channeled it outward, focusing on the pathogen, willing it to halt, to dissolve.

The air around her shifted, the smoke curling and pulling toward her like iron filings to a magnet. She gritted her teeth, her body trembling as the strain mounted. Every cell in her body screamed in protest, her vision dimming at the edges.

"Lily!" Ethan's voice was sharper now, his fear palpable. "You're pushing too hard!"

"I have to," she gasped, her knees buckling. "I can't stop now."

The energy intensified, a blinding light emanating from her hands as the pathogen condensed, folding in on itself. The room vibrated with an almost deafening hum, the tension thick enough to choke on. Lily's breaths came in ragged gasps, her body threatening to collapse under the weight of her effort.

Finally, with a final, desperate push, the light exploded outward, filling the room with a brilliant white glow. The pathogen's presence vanished, the air clearing as if a storm had passed.

Lily crumpled to the floor, her body limp, her breath shallow. Ethan was at her side in an instant, his hand pressing against her cheek. "Lily, stay with me. Open your eyes."

She forced them open, her gaze meeting his. "Did… did it work?"

He nodded, his voice thick with emotion. "Yeah, Doc. You did it. You stopped it."

A faint smile tugged at her lips as exhaustion claimed her. "Good. Now it's your turn to finish this."

Her eyes fluttered shut, and Ethan gathered her into his arms, his jaw set with determination. The fight wasn't over yet, but Lily had given them a chance. And he wasn't about to waste it.

Chapter 14
The Breaking Point

The lab was eerily silent, the calm after the storm. Lily stood in the center, her hands trembling as she stared at the equipment before her. The pathogen wasn't just contained; it was waiting, like a predator poised to strike again. She inhaled deeply, the weight of responsibility pressing on her shoulders as she prepared to do what had to be done.

Behind her, Ethan leaned against the counter, his hand pressed to his injured side. Despite the strain etched across his face, his eyes never wavered from her. "You've got this, Lily."

She glanced at him, her lips pressing into a thin line. "Do I? Because right now, it feels like I'm holding the world together with duct tape and a prayer."

"You're doing a hell of a lot more than that," he said, his voice steady despite his exhaustion. "Look at what you've done already. You stopped the release. You contained the pathogen. Now you finish it."

She turned back to the terminal, her fingers flying over the keyboard. "Easier said than done. Neutralizing this thing means breaking it down at the cellular level. One wrong move, and it could mutate into something worse."

"Then don't make the wrong move," he said simply, the faintest hint of a smirk on his lips.

She let out a shaky laugh, shaking her head. "You make it sound so easy."

"It's not," he admitted, stepping closer. "But if anyone can figure it out, it's you."

Her chest tightened, the warmth in his words cutting through her fear. She exhaled slowly, her focus narrowing as she pulled up the pathogen's structural data. The screen was a dizzying array of molecular diagrams and chemical formulas. She studied it intently, her mind racing.

"This pathogen is engineered to adapt," she murmured, more to herself than to Ethan. "Its proteins are designed to bond with human cells almost instantly. But if I can destabilize the protein chains, it'll collapse on itself."

Ethan's brow furrowed as he watched her work. "And how do you do that?"

"With heat," she said, her fingers darting toward the equipment. "Controlled thermal exposure can unravel the proteins without triggering mutation. But it has to be precise."

She grabbed a set of syringes filled with stabilizing agents and moved toward the incubator. Ethan stepped forward, his concern evident. "You sure about this?"

"No," she admitted, her voice tight. "But it's our best shot."

As she loaded the samples into the incubator, the machine beeped softly, its screen displaying the temperature settings. She hesitated, her hand hovering over the controls.

"What's wrong?" Ethan asked, stepping beside her.

"If the temperature fluctuates, even by a fraction of a degree…" She trailed off, shaking her head. "I could trigger a reaction we can't control."

Ethan placed a hand on her shoulder, grounding her. "Then don't let it fluctuate. You've got this, Lily. Trust yourself."

She glanced at him, her chest tightening. "You have way too much faith in me."

"I have exactly the right amount," he said, his voice firm. "Now do what you do best."

She nodded, her focus sharpening. Taking a deep breath, she keyed in the temperature settings and hit start. The incubator whirred to life, the faint hum vibrating through the room. Lily watched the monitor, her pulse racing as the temperature began to climb.

Ethan stood beside her, his presence steady and reassuring. "What happens now?"

"Now we wait," she said, her voice barely above a whisper. "If the proteins destabilize, the pathogen will degrade into inert compounds. If not…"

He finished her thought. "We figure it out."

Minutes stretched into an eternity as the temperature stabilized, the screen displaying a countdown. Lily's hands gripped the edge of the counter, her knuckles white. Ethan leaned closer, his voice breaking the silence.

"You're not alone in this," he said softly.

She glanced at him, her eyes glistening with unspoken emotion. "I know. And that's the only reason I'm still standing."

He smiled faintly, his voice tinged with warmth. "Good. Because I'm not going anywhere."

The monitor beeped, drawing their attention. Lily's breath hitched as the display updated. The pathogen's protein chains began to unravel, the molecular structures collapsing in real-time.

"It's working," she whispered, her voice filled with awe. "It's actually working."

Ethan let out a low laugh, his relief evident. "Told you."

She shot him a wry look, her tension easing slightly. "You're insufferable."

"And you're brilliant," he countered.

The final seconds ticked down, and the incubator emitted a soft chime. Lily pulled the samples out, inspecting them closely. The once-dangerous liquid was now inert, its deadly potential neutralized.

"It's done," she said, her voice trembling with a mix of exhaustion and triumph. "We did it."

Ethan placed a hand on her back, his smile faint but genuine. "No, you did it, Doc. I was just here to cheer you on."

She turned to him, her eyes shining with gratitude. "I couldn't have done it without you."

He smirked, his voice soft. "Good thing you didn't have to."

For the first time in hours, Lily felt the weight on her shoulders begin to lift. The fight wasn't over yet, but this victory—this moment—was theirs. Together, they had done the impossible.

The lab was a pressure cooker, every second stretching into eternity as Lily worked feverishly over the terminal. The incubator hummed behind her, its contents on the verge of neutralization. Ethan was at her side, his sharp breaths betraying the pain from his injury, but his focus remained locked on the doorway, waiting for the inevitable.

"They're going to come for us," Ethan said, his voice low. "Harlow's not the type to let this go."

"I know," Lily replied, her voice tight as she navigated the labyrinth of commands on the screen. "Just a little longer. If I can stabilize this last sequence…"

The sound of footsteps echoed from the hallway, loud and purposeful. Ethan's posture stiffened, his hand instinctively moving to the rod he'd salvaged earlier. "They're here."

The lab door burst open, and two of Harlow's guards stormed in, their movements deliberate and menacing. Behind them, Harlow's voice rang out, sharp and cold. "I told you, Dr. Chen. You can't win."

Ethan stepped forward, his stance defensive as he placed himself between Lily and the guards. "Funny, looks like we're doing just fine."

Harlow entered, his expression dark as he gestured toward the guards. "Deal with him. Dr. Chen and I have unfinished business."

One of the guards lunged at Ethan, but Ethan met him head-on, his movements precise despite the pain evident in his every step. Lily's hands trembled as she kept typing, her focus split between the escalating fight and the terminal. "I can't do this if you're—"

"You can," Ethan interrupted, blocking a swing and countering with a sharp jab to the guard's stomach. "Just finish it!"

The second guard moved toward Lily, but before he could reach her, a shot rang out. The room froze as the guard dropped to his knees, clutching his shoulder. All eyes turned to the doorway, where Detective Jordan Reeves stood, his gun raised and his expression calm but resolute.

"Looks like I made it just in time," Reeves said, stepping inside. "I was starting to think you didn't want my help."

Lily's heart leapt, a wave of relief crashing over her. "Reeves! How did you—"

"Follow the trail of chaos you left behind," he said with a faint smirk. "You're not exactly subtle, Doc."

Harlow's eyes narrowed, his voice dripping with disdain. "Detective Reeves. Always a step behind."

"Not today," Reeves said, his gun trained on Harlow. "Hands where I can see them."

Harlow raised his hands, his calm demeanor cracking just slightly. "Do you even know what you're interrupting? The work being done here will change the course of humanity."

"Yeah, you keep telling yourself that," Reeves said, his voice steady. "All I see is a madman playing God."

The remaining guard hesitated, glancing between Harlow and Reeves. Ethan seized the moment, landing a sharp blow that sent the man sprawling. He turned to Reeves, his breathing labored but his gratitude clear. "Took you long enough."

Reeves gave him a quick nod. "Nice to see you too, Wilde."

Lily's fingers moved faster now, her focus sharpening with the tension momentarily eased. The terminal beeped, and the final command executed. She exhaled sharply, relief flooding her as the monitor displayed a green message: **Pathogen Neutralized.**

"It's done," she said, turning to face the others. "We've neutralized it."

Harlow's expression darkened, his hands balling into fists. "You have no idea what you've just destroyed."

"I know exactly what I destroyed," Lily shot back, her voice steady despite the adrenaline coursing through her. "Your weapon. Your plan. Everything."

Reeves moved toward Harlow, his gun still raised. "It's over, Harlow. You're coming with me."

Harlow sneered, his eyes darting toward the equipment. "You think you've won? This is just one lab. There are others—"

Ethan stepped forward, his voice cold and sharp. "And we'll find them. But you won't be around to see it."

Reeves pulled a pair of handcuffs from his belt, securing Harlow with practiced efficiency. "You can tell your sob story to the courts. I'm sure they'll love hearing about your grand vision."

Lily sagged against the counter, the weight of the moment finally catching up with her. Ethan was at her side in an instant, his hand resting on her back. "You okay?"

"I will be," she said, her voice quiet but firm. "Thanks to both of you."

Reeves glanced at her, his expression softening. "You did the hard part, Doc. I just made sure you had the time to do it."

She managed a faint smile, her exhaustion mingling with gratitude. "You made all the difference."

As Reeves led Harlow out of the lab, the room fell into a heavy silence. Lily turned to Ethan, her chest tightening at the sight of him leaning heavily against the counter.

"We did it," she said, her voice breaking slightly.

"We did," he agreed, his smirk faint but genuine. "And you were incredible."

For the first time in what felt like hours, Lily allowed herself to breathe. The fight wasn't over, not completely—but for now, they had won a battle that felt impossible. Together, they had faced the storm and come out stronger for it.

The hum of the lab equipment was deafening in the heavy silence that followed Harlow's capture. Lily stood at the terminal, her body trembling as exhaustion crept into her limbs.

The pathogen was neutralized, but the containment process was still ongoing, a delicate balance that required every ounce of focus she had left.

Ethan moved to her side, his steps unsteady but determined. "How much longer?"

"Not long," she said, her voice faint. "I just need to stabilize the containment fields. If I can reinforce the molecular barriers, we can secure the pathogen completely."

Ethan leaned against the counter, his eyes scanning her pale face. "Lily, you're barely standing. Let me—"

"You can't," she interrupted, shaking her head. "This isn't something you can fight, Ethan. It's science, and it's…" Her voice faltered as a wave of dizziness hit her. She gripped the edge of the counter, breathing hard.

"Lily," he said sharply, stepping closer to steady her. His hands gripped her shoulders, grounding her. "You can't do this if you're collapsing. Just breathe."

"I don't have time to breathe," she snapped, though her voice lacked its usual strength. "If I stop now, everything we've done will mean nothing. I have to finish this."

"And you will," he said, his tone firm but gentle. "But you're not doing it alone."

She glanced at him, her chest tightening at the intensity in his gaze. "Ethan, I—"

"You don't have to say it," he cut her off, his voice softening. "I know. And I'm not going anywhere. Whatever happens, I'm here."

Her breath hitched, the weight of his words settling over her like a balm. She nodded, her voice trembling. "Then help me keep it together."

He smirked faintly, his hands steadying her as she turned back to the terminal. "Always."

She forced herself to focus, her fingers moving over the keyboard with mechanical precision. The containment field flickered on the screen, its stability wavering. "It's not enough," she murmured, frustration creeping into her voice. "The pathogen's too volatile. It's fighting the barriers."

"Then give it hell," Ethan said simply, his confidence unwavering.

A faint laugh escaped her, and she shook her head. "You make it sound so easy."

"It is," he replied, leaning closer. "Because I believe in you, Doc. You've got this."

Her throat tightened, and she nodded, drawing strength from his presence. Closing her eyes, she took a deep breath, reaching deep into the core of her abilities. The heat returned, spreading through her veins like liquid fire, her biomancy responding to her call.

"I can feel it," she whispered, her voice barely audible.

Ethan's brow furrowed. "Feel what?"

"The pathogen," she said, her hands trembling as she extended them toward the terminal. "It's still alive, still trying to break through. But I can hold it."

His hand covered hers, steadying her. "Then hold it, Lily. I'm right here."

The room seemed to blur at the edges as she focused all her energy on the containment field. The pathogen's chaotic energy pulsed through her senses, a writhing, malevolent force that resisted her every move. She gritted her teeth, her body trembling under the strain.

"It's too much," she gasped, her voice breaking. "I can't—"

"Yes, you can," Ethan interrupted, his voice sharp and resolute. "You've already done the impossible. This is just one more step."

Her breath came in short, ragged bursts, but she nodded, his words anchoring her. She pushed harder, her abilities surging as she funneled every ounce of strength into the field. The pathogen's resistance faltered, its energy dimming.

"It's working," she said, her voice shaking with relief. "The barriers are holding."

Ethan's hand squeezed hers, his voice softening. "You're incredible, you know that?"

She let out a breathless laugh, her exhaustion evident. "Tell me that after we survive this."

The screen flashed green, a chime signaling the final containment lock. The pathogen's energy disappeared, its destructive force neutralized at last. Lily sagged against the counter, her knees threatening to give out.

"You did it," Ethan said, his voice filled with quiet pride.

"We did it," she corrected, her lips curving into a faint smile.

He wrapped an arm around her shoulders, his strength steadying her. "You're going to be okay, Lily."

She met his gaze, her exhaustion mingling with gratitude. "Not without you."

"Good thing I'm not going anywhere," he said, his voice warm despite the weariness in his eyes.

As the weight of their accomplishment settled over them, the lab grew quiet again. The fight wasn't over—there were still questions to answer, loose ends to tie up—but for now, they had won. Together, they had faced the impossible and emerged stronger for it.

And that, Lily thought, was a victory worth everything.

The lab was quiet now, the once-persistent alarms silenced, leaving only the soft hum of the containment field. The pathogen was neutralized, locked behind layers of reinforced barriers. Lily stood at the center of the room, her breathing shallow, her body trembling with exhaustion. The faint glow of the containment unit cast long shadows across her face, highlighting the lines of weariness and relief etched there.

Ethan approached her slowly, his steps unsteady, his hand still pressed against his injured side. "It's done."

She turned to him, her expression unreadable. For a moment, she didn't speak, her eyes scanning his face as though searching for reassurance. Finally, she nodded, her voice barely above a whisper. "It's done."

He reached out, his hand brushing her arm lightly. "You okay?"

"Am I okay?" she repeated, a hollow laugh escaping her lips. She shook her head, her voice trembling. "I don't even know what that means anymore."

Ethan's brow furrowed, concern flickering in his eyes. "Lily…"

She stepped away, wrapping her arms around herself. "I just—I don't know what I've become, Ethan. What I've done." Her voice broke, the weight of the past hours crashing over her. "I used something inside me, something I barely understand, and I could've killed us all if I'd messed up."

"But you didn't," he said firmly, his voice cutting through her spiral. "You stopped the pathogen. You saved lives."

"At what cost?" she snapped, her eyes flashing with a mix of anger and anguish. "I crossed every line I swore I never would. I risked everything—my ethics, my health, my humanity—and for what? A victory that feels like a loss?"

Ethan stepped closer, his presence steadying. "You crossed those lines because you had to. Because no one else could've done what you did."

She shook her head, tears welling in her eyes. "You don't understand. I don't even recognize myself right now. The person I've become…"

"I do understand," he interrupted, his tone soft but resolute. "I've been there, Lily. Standing on the edge, wondering if the choices I made were worth the cost. And you know what I learned?"

She didn't respond, her gaze fixed on the floor.

"I learned that it's not about the lines you cross," he continued. "It's about why you crossed them. You did this because it mattered. Because people's lives were on the line, and you were the only one who could make a difference."

Her lips trembled, but she didn't speak. He reached out again, his hand finding hers and squeezing gently.

"You didn't do this alone," he said, his voice quieter now. "You had me. And Reeves. And every person who believed in you, whether you saw it or not. You don't carry this weight alone, Lily."

Her throat tightened, and she looked up at him, her eyes glistening. "It doesn't feel that way."

"I know," he said, his gaze steady. "But that's why I'm here. To remind you that you don't have to face this alone."

She exhaled shakily, her hand gripping his like a lifeline. "I'm so tired, Ethan."

"I know," he said softly. "But you did it. You stopped something that could've destroyed everything. That has to mean something."

She nodded slowly, the tears finally spilling over. He pulled her into a gentle embrace, his arms steady despite his own exhaustion. She clung to him, the weight of the moment crashing over her in waves.

For a long time, they stood there in silence, the room around them a testament to the battle they had fought. Broken equipment, shattered glass, and the faint glow of the containment unit—it all spoke of the chaos they had endured. But amidst the wreckage, there was peace.

Eventually, she pulled back, her expression softening as she looked at him. "You're hurt," she said, her voice quiet but firm. "We need to get you patched up."

He smirked faintly, the corner of his mouth lifting. "I'll live. You're the one I'm worried about."

"I'll be okay," she said, though her tone wavered. "Eventually."

"Good," he said, his smile widening slightly. "Because we've still got a lot of work to do."

She laughed softly, shaking her head. "Of course we do."

As they left the lab, the enormity of what they had accomplished lingered between them. The victory was real, but so was the cost. They had faced the impossible and come out the other side, but neither of them would ever be the same.

And yet, as they walked side by side, their steps slow but purposeful, there was a quiet understanding between them—a bond forged in fire, stronger than anything they had faced before. They weren't done fighting. But for the first time, they knew they could face whatever came next. Together.

Chapter 15
The Final Showdown

The tension in the air was palpable as Lily pushed open the heavy wooden door to Dr. Vega's office, her breath coming in shallow bursts. Ethan followed close behind, his expression hard, his movements deliberate. The sterile lighting of the hospital seemed to dim in this room, casting long shadows across the mahogany desk and leather-bound books lining the shelves. Dr. Vega sat at her desk, a calm smile playing on her lips as if she had been expecting them.

"Well," Vega said, leaning back in her chair, her fingers steepled. "This is a surprise. To what do I owe the pleasure?"

Ethan stepped forward, his voice cold and cutting. "It's over."

Vega's smile widened slightly, her demeanor unbothered. "You'll have to be more specific, Mr. Wilde. Over is such a vague term."

Lily's hand tightened around the folder she carried, the weight of the evidence inside feeling heavier than it should. She stepped to Ethan's side, her voice trembling but determined. "We know what you've been doing. The tests, the infections, the deaths. It's all here." She slapped the folder onto the desk.

Vega barely glanced at it. "And?"

"And?" Lily repeated, her voice rising. "This is illegal! You've been experimenting on patients, using this hospital as your personal lab. People have died because of you!"

Vega's calm demeanor didn't waver. If anything, she seemed amused. "You're quite passionate, Dr. Chen. I admire that. But you're missing the bigger picture."

Ethan's jaw tightened, and he took another step closer. "The bigger picture? Is that what you tell yourself to sleep at night? That it's all for some greater good?"

Vega tilted her head, her eyes sharp and calculating. "Do you think the world is as black and white as that? Sacrifices must be made, Mr. Wilde. You, of all people, should understand that."

"I understand the difference between sacrifice and murder," Ethan shot back.

"Murder?" Vega echoed, feigning shock. "How dramatic. Tell me, did you feel this way when you were on the other side? Or was it easier when you could pretend your actions were justified?"

Ethan's fists clenched at his sides, but he didn't rise to the bait. Instead, he nodded toward the folder. "It's all there. The unauthorized tests, the falsified records, the trail of patients you used and discarded. This ends now."

Vega chuckled, the sound low and condescending. "And what do you plan to do with your little folder of evidence? Take it to Dr. Harlow? The board? Do you honestly think they'll touch this? They're complicit, whether they know it or not."

Lily's stomach churned at Vega's words, but she refused to back down. "We're taking it to the authorities. The police, the press—whoever will listen. You won't get away with this."

"Oh, Lily," Vega said, her tone almost pitying. "Do you think I haven't prepared for this? A few files won't be enough to bring me down. I'm part of something much larger than this hospital, something you can't even begin to comprehend."

"Then enlighten us," Ethan said, his voice like steel.

Vega stood, her movements slow and deliberate. She walked around the desk, her heels clicking against the polished floor. "You think you're heroes, don't you? Coming in here, demanding justice, acting as though you have any real power. But you're just pawns in a much bigger game. A game that's been played long before you stepped into this hospital."

"You're stalling," Ethan said, his tone sharp. "We're not here for your speeches."

Vega smirked. "And yet, here you are, listening."

Lily stepped forward, her voice trembling with anger. "We're here because people deserve better than this. They deserve better than you."

Vega's expression hardened slightly, a flicker of something unreadable passing through her eyes. "And what do you think will happen if you expose this? The world will clap for you? Call you heroes? No. They'll bury you. Just like they bury everyone who gets in their way."

"We'll take that risk," Ethan said firmly.

Vega's gaze shifted between them, her smirk returning. "Brave words. But bravery doesn't win wars. Power does."

Lily felt a chill run down her spine as Vega stepped back behind her desk, her calm, unrepentant demeanor more unsettling than outright rage.

"You won't get away with this," Lily said again, her voice steady despite the fear creeping in.

"We'll see," Vega replied, her tone almost playful.

As Ethan and Lily turned to leave, the weight of the encounter settled heavily over them. The evidence in their hands was damning, but Vega's confidence unnerved Lily more than she wanted to admit.

"This isn't over," Ethan said quietly as they stepped into the hallway.

"No," Lily agreed, clutching the folder tightly. "But it's a start."

The ER, once a haven of controlled chaos, now felt like a war zone. Armed operatives in tactical gear moved through the hospital in coordinated teams, their movements efficient and deliberate. The air was thick with tension as staff and patients were ushered into secure areas, their confused and frightened faces adding to the growing unease.

In the makeshift lab Lily had set up in a secluded corner of the hospital, she bent over a microscope, her gloved hands steady despite the adrenaline coursing through her veins. The samples in front of her—blood, mucus, and tissue from the infected patients—were a jigsaw puzzle she had to solve before it was too late.

Ethan stood by the door, his arms crossed, his posture calm but alert. His dark eyes scanned the room, lingering on Lily as she worked.

"How's it coming?" he asked, his voice cutting through the hum of the nearby equipment.

"It's not," Lily snapped without looking up. "The pathogen's mutating faster than I can track. Every time I think I've got a handle on it, it changes."

Ethan stepped closer, his tone calm but firm. "You're doing fine, Doc. Just keep going. We've got your back."

Lily straightened, pulling off her gloves with a frustrated sigh. "Having my back doesn't mean much if I can't figure this out. We're running out of time, Ethan."

Before he could respond, the radio clipped to his vest crackled to life. "Team Bravo, report. West wing is clear. No sign of secondary targets."

"Copy that," Ethan said into the radio. He turned back to Lily, his gaze steady. "Focus on the samples. Let us worry about the rest."

She hesitated, her eyes meeting his. "This isn't just about the samples, Ethan. If this spreads—"

"It won't," he interrupted, his tone resolute. "Not if you do your job."

The words, though blunt, were grounding. Lily nodded, slipping on a new pair of gloves and leaning back over the microscope. "Alright," she muttered. "Let's try this again."

The tension in the room thickened as the minutes ticked by. Ethan stayed close, his presence a steadying force as Lily worked.

"I need you to run interference," she said suddenly, pulling a syringe of plasma from the rack.

Ethan frowned. "What kind of interference?"

"The pathogen's targeting specific genetic markers," she explained quickly. "If I can isolate the common factor, I can create a targeted treatment. But I need more samples—recent ones."

He nodded, already moving toward the door. "I'll get them."

"Be careful," she called after him, but he was already gone.

The lab door swung open ten minutes later, and Ethan strode in carrying a cooler packed with vials of fresh samples. His jacket was smeared with dirt and something dark Lily didn't want to identify, but his expression was focused.

"Got what you need?" he asked, setting the cooler on the counter.

Lily opened it, her breath catching at the sight of the blood samples neatly labeled and packed. "This might do it," she said, pulling out a vial.

"Good," Ethan said, leaning against the counter. "Now work your magic."

She shot him a look but didn't argue, sliding the sample under the microscope. "If this doesn't work…"

"It will," Ethan said firmly.

"How can you be so sure?"

"Because you don't give up," he replied, his tone softening. "And I've seen you pull off miracles before."

His words, unexpected and earnest, made her pause. She glanced at him, her frustration giving way to something closer to gratitude. "Thanks," she said quietly.

"Don't thank me yet," he replied with a faint smirk.

The lab fell into silence again, save for the hum of equipment and the faint clicks of Lily's tools. She worked methodically, her focus laser-sharp. Ethan stayed close, his presence grounding her as she fought to stay ahead of the pathogen's relentless mutations.

Finally, after what felt like hours, Lily straightened, holding up a vial of pale yellow liquid. "This is it," she said, her voice trembling with a mix of relief and exhaustion. "The counteragent. It should neutralize the pathogen."

Ethan stepped forward, his expression unreadable. "You're sure?"

"No," she admitted. "But it's the best shot we've got."

He nodded, taking the vial from her and holding it up to the light. "Then let's end this."

The ER was eerily quiet in the aftermath. The steady hum of machines and the occasional murmur of voices felt more oppressive than comforting. Lily sat in a stiff-backed chair outside the hospital administrator's office, her fingers laced together tightly in her lap. Her white coat, once pristine, was stained and crumpled, a testament to the battle she had just fought.

The door opened, and Dr. Harlow stepped out, his face a mask of frustration. He paused, his eyes narrowing slightly as they met Lily's.

"They're ready for you," he said, his tone clipped.

Lily stood, her legs unsteady beneath her. As she entered the office, the weight of the moment settled over her. Four faces stared back at her from behind a polished oak table, their expressions ranging from curiosity to outright skepticism.

"Dr. Chen," the lead administrator began, her tone cool. "You've had quite a night."

Lily nodded, her voice catching in her throat. "Yes, ma'am."

The administrator leaned forward, her hands folded neatly on the table. "You want to explain how you, a first-year attending, found yourself at the center of an unauthorized operation involving armed operatives and a pathogen threat?"

Lily hesitated, her mind racing. She couldn't tell them everything—she wasn't sure they would believe her even if she did.

"I did what I thought was necessary to save lives," she said carefully.

"Necessary?" another administrator echoed, his voice laced with incredulity. "You coordinated with outside forces, bypassed hospital protocol, and exposed this institution to liabilities we can't even begin to calculate."

"Those 'outside forces' stopped a pathogen from spreading through this hospital and possibly beyond," Lily said, her voice steadying. "If I hadn't acted, more people would have died."

"And yet," the lead administrator said, her gaze piercing, "you didn't bring any of this to your supervisors. Why?"

Lily swallowed hard. "Because I didn't think they would listen."

The tension in the room thickened.

"Thank you, Dr. Chen," the administrator said finally. "You're dismissed. We'll be in touch regarding our decision."

Lily nodded, her throat too tight to speak. She turned and left the room, the sound of the door closing behind her echoing in her ears.

Ethan was waiting for her in the corridor, leaning casually against the wall. He straightened as she approached, his dark eyes scanning her face.

"How'd it go?" he asked, his tone light but his expression serious.

"They're deciding whether or not to fire me," Lily said bluntly, the exhaustion in her voice impossible to miss.

"They won't," Ethan said with quiet confidence.

"You don't know that," she replied, her frustration bubbling to the surface. "This hospital doesn't want a scandal. They'll do whatever it takes to save face—even if it means making me the scapegoat."

Ethan stepped closer, his voice softening. "You did the right thing, Lily. That's what matters."

She shook her head, her eyes stinging. "I don't even know if it was the right thing. People died, Ethan. And now…" Her voice broke, and she looked away. "I don't even know what I've got left."

"You've got a lot more than you think," he said firmly. "You stopped this thing from spreading. You saved lives, even if it doesn't feel like it right now."

Lily's gaze flicked back to him, her expression hard. "And what about you? What happens to you now?"

Ethan smirked faintly, but it didn't reach his eyes. "I disappear, like I always do."

"That's not fair," she said, the words slipping out before she could stop them.

"Fair doesn't matter, Doc," he said, his tone lighter than the moment deserved. "What matters is that the people who needed help got it."

She stared at him, her frustration giving way to a deep, aching sadness. "And what about the people who helped? What about you?"

Ethan hesitated, his smirk fading. "I'll be fine, Lily. I always am."

The weight of his words settled over her, and for a moment, neither of them spoke.

"Thank you," she said finally, her voice barely above a whisper.

Ethan nodded, his expression softening. "Take care of yourself, Doc. You're not like anyone else in this place. Don't forget that."

With that, he turned and walked away, his footsteps fading into the distance.

Lily watched him go, a mix of emotions swirling in her chest. The hospital was quiet again, but the echoes of the past few hours would linger for a long time.

She took a deep breath, squaring her shoulders as she prepared to return to the ER. Whatever came next, she wasn't going to back down.

The ER was uncharacteristically still, the lull after chaos settling like a thin fog over the space. Lily stood near the nurse's station, her hands resting lightly on the counter. The monitors still beeped, and the occasional murmur of voices added to the heavy silence, but the usual rush of activity had faded.

She glanced toward the entrance, half-expecting Ethan to reappear, leaning casually against the doorframe with that smirk of his. But she knew better. He was gone, just as he said he would be, slipping into the shadows as easily as he'd stepped out of them.

"Earth to Dr. Chen."

Lily turned at the sound of Nina's voice. The charge nurse leaned against the counter, her expression curious but gentle.

"You've been staring at that door for five minutes," Nina said, her tone teasing. "Expecting someone?"

"No," Lily replied quickly, shaking her head. "Just… thinking."

"About the insanity of the last few days?" Nina asked, her voice dropping slightly. "Because, honestly, I'm still wrapping my head around it."

"Yeah," Lily said softly. "Something like that."

Nina studied her for a moment before giving a small nod. "Well, whatever's going on in that head of yours, don't forget to eat. You look like you're about to keel over."

Lily smiled faintly. "Thanks, Nina."

As Nina walked away, Lily's gaze drifted back to the entrance. The weight of the past few days pressed down on her, a mixture of relief, exhaustion, and something she couldn't quite name. She had always thought of herself as steady, unshakable in her purpose. But now? Now she felt like a completely different person.

The faint creak of the glass doors opening snapped her out of her thoughts. She turned instinctively, but it wasn't Ethan. Just a man in a business suit, his face pale and tired as he approached the reception desk.

Lily exhaled, her chest tightening with a pang of disappointment she wasn't ready to admit. Later, she stood in the break room, staring out the window at the sprawling cityscape beyond. The sun was beginning to rise, casting a soft golden hue over the buildings. The view, once familiar and comforting, now felt different—charged with possibility and uncertainty.

The door behind her creaked open, and she didn't need to turn to know who it was.

"You're still here?" Nina asked, stepping inside with two cups of coffee.

"Couldn't sleep," Lily replied, taking the cup Nina offered her.

"Can't blame you," Nina said, leaning against the counter. "After everything that's happened, I don't think I'll sleep for a week."

Lily chuckled softly, the sound tinged with weariness. "You're not alone."

They stood in silence for a moment, the quiet punctuated only by the faint hum of the refrigerator.

"You did good, you know," Nina said finally, her voice sincere. "I don't know everything that went down, but you held it together. You made a difference."

Lily glanced at her, a small smile tugging at her lips. "Thanks, Nina. That means a lot."

Nina nodded, her gaze thoughtful. "Just don't make a habit of saving the world, alright? We need you here."

Lily's smile widened slightly. "I'll try to keep that in mind."

As Nina left, Lily returned her gaze to the window. The city stretched out before her, vast and full of unknowns. The mystery at St. Raphael's might have been over, but it felt more like the closing of one chapter than the end of the story.

She thought of Ethan—his cryptic warnings, his steady presence, and the unspoken truths that still lingered between them. He had left without fanfare, but his words stayed with her: *You're not like anyone else here.*

For better or worse, he had been right. She wasn't the same person she had been when she walked through the doors of this hospital.

Lily took a deep breath, her reflection staring back at her in the glass. The scars of the past days ran deep, but they weren't the kind that made her feel weaker. If anything, they had made her stronger.

"This is just the beginning," she murmured to herself, her voice steady. The city outside seemed to glimmer in agreement, the dawn casting a hopeful glow over its endless possibilities.

The stillness of the moment was interrupted by the soft buzz of her pager. She glanced at it, the familiar sense of duty pulling her back to the present. It was a call for a new patient—something routine, but necessary.

Straightening her shoulders, Lily set her coffee down and stepped out of the break room. The quiet ER was beginning to stir again, signs of life returning to its familiar rhythm. As she walked toward the nurse's station, she realized that even amidst the lingering shadows of the past, the work here was far from over.

And neither was she.

Epilogue
Shadows in the Light

The world outside St. Raphael's Hospital was still recovering. The aftermath of the bioweapon conspiracy had left scars—on the city, the patients, and everyone caught in its web. For Lily Chen, the days following the revelation felt surreal, as though she were navigating the hospital corridors in a fog.

The media frenzy had descended almost immediately after the arrest of Dr. Vega and the exposure of the covert operation. News vans clogged the streets outside, reporters jostling for statements from hospital staff. Lily avoided the cameras, retreating into the rhythm of patient care, where she felt most grounded. She couldn't avoid the whispers, though. Colleagues gave her a wide berth in the hallways, their conversations halting when she approached. Some looked at her with respect, others with suspicion, as though her role in uncovering the conspiracy made her complicit in its horrors.

It was a weight she hadn't anticipated.

In the quiet hours of the evening, she often found herself in the break room, staring at the glow of her phone. Ethan had disappeared the night the operation ended. True to form, there had been no grand farewell, no lingering goodbye. Just a folded note tucked into her locker.

*"Lily,
You were right to trust your instincts. I'm sorry for dragging

you into this, but I never could have done it without you. You're stronger than you know. Stay that way.

—E.W."*

She had read it so many times the creases in the paper had worn thin. Part of her had expected it—Ethan was never meant to stay—but his absence left a void nonetheless.

One night, she found herself standing in the now-deserted Infectious Disease Wing. The door to the restricted area hung slightly ajar, the keypad dark and unresponsive. The room felt lifeless, stripped of the secrets and tension that had once defined it. Still, as she stepped inside, a shiver ran down her spine.

Her thoughts drifted to Margaret Fields and the other patients who had unknowingly become pawns in a deadly experiment. Most had recovered, but some had not been so lucky. Lily had tried to visit Margaret several times, only to be told that she had been transferred out of St. Raphael's under government supervision. No one would tell her more.

"They're protecting her," Ethan had said during one of their final conversations. "Or, at least, that's what they'll tell themselves."

The thought lingered, an unanswered question she wasn't sure she wanted to chase.

Weeks later, Lily was called into Dr. Harlow's office. The usually disheveled physician sat behind his desk, his expression uncharacteristically serious. A letter rested between them, its crisp envelope marked with a government insignia.

“You’ve made waves, Dr. Chen,” Harlow said, his voice neutral. “This came for you.”

Lily frowned, her pulse quickening as she reached for the envelope. Inside was a letter inviting her to participate in a classified debriefing with federal investigators. Her role in uncovering the bioweapon plot had not gone unnoticed.

“What does this mean?” she asked, her voice quieter than she intended.

Harlow leaned back, studying her with a rare intensity. “It means you have a choice to make. You can stay here, keep your head down, and rebuild your career. Or you can step into a world where this kind of thing happens more often than you’d like to think.”

Lily left the office with the letter tucked into her coat pocket, her mind a whirlwind of possibilities. She had spent her entire career believing in the sanctity of patient care, the importance of healing above all else. But the events of the past months had shown her a darker side of medicine—a place where healing was a weapon and trust was a commodity.

That night, she returned to her apartment, the weight of the decision pressing heavily on her. As she set the letter on her coffee table, her phone buzzed with a new message. The number was unlisted, but the words were unmistakably his:

"The world needs people like you, Lily. People who ask questions. If you choose to keep asking, I'll be here. —E.W."

For the first time in weeks, she smiled.

In the days that followed, Lily continued her work in the ER, but the letter never left her bag. She wasn't ready to decide—not yet. But as she treated her patients, listened to their fears, and watched the world recover from the shadows of what had nearly happened, she felt something new stirring within her: a sense of purpose that went beyond the hospital walls.

Perhaps Ethan was right. Perhaps the world needed people who asked questions. And perhaps it was time for her to stop fearing the answers.

As she stepped out into the crisp evening air, the city lights glittering like stars above her, Lily Chen took a deep breath. The scars of the past were still fresh, but they no longer felt like a burden. They felt like a beginning.

Milton Keynes UK
Ingram Content Group UK Ltd.
UKHW031342011224
451755UK00001B/209

9 798230 621959